Forced Alliance

Center Point
Large Print

Also by Lenora Worth and available from Center Point Large Print:

Diamond Secret
In Pursuit of a Princess

**This Large Print Book carries the
Seal of Approval of N.A.V.H.**

Forced Alliance

Lenora Worth

CENTER POINT LARGE PRINT
THORNDIKE, MAINE

This Center Point Large Print edition is published
in the year 2014 by arrangement with
Harlequin Books S.A.

The text of this Large Print edition is unabridged.
In other aspects, this book may vary
from the original edition.
Printed in the United States of America
on permanent paper.
Set in 16-point Times New Roman type.

ISBN: 978-1-62899-372-1

Library of Congress Cataloging-in-Publication Data

Worth, Lenora.
Forced alliance / Lenora Worth. — Center Point Large Print edition.
pages ; cm
Summary: "FBI agent Josie Gilbert is forced to take her confidential
informant Connor Randall into hiding without blowing his cover when
the crime boss they are trying to take down becomes a target. Dodging
hit-men and fighting attraction, she must determine if she can trust
Connor or if he is working another con"—Provided by publisher.
ISBN 978-1-62899-372-1 (library binding : alk. paper)
1. Large type books. I. Title.
PS3573.O6965F67 2014
813'.54—dc23
                                                        2014034524

To Shiny—with many thanks :)

Keep thy heart with all diligence:
for out of it are the issues of life.
—*Proverbs* 4:23

ONE . . .

A glint of light pushed through the skyscraper-gray dusk, allowing the sun to offer one more ray of hope to the city of New Orleans before the hungry, humid night engulfed it in shadows. Just as that sun slipped behind the tall buildings up and down Canal Street, a muffled shot hissed downward through the air and made contact with human flesh.

At about the same time, Connor Randall adjusted his formal bow tie and stepped out of a still-purring black sports car. Holding the car door away from the sweating valet, Connor looked up and around, old habits dying hard.

And he spotted none other than Louis Armond standing a few yards away, the unmoving body of a beautiful blonde lying still by his feet. The Mafia king's shocked gaze zigzagged up in a jagged path. He drew a weapon and pivoted in a nervous circle before he fell down on his knees and pulled the unconscious woman into his arms. His olive-skinned face twisted in grief and terror. Then he glanced around until his scowl hit on Connor and stopped.

Connor got back in his car and peeled out of

the parking garage. He reached Armond, shifted down and hit the brakes. "Get in," he called. "Mr. Armond, get in the car."

FBI Special Agent Josie Gilbert's cell rang at the same time she was about to bite into her first slice of veggie pizza. Still holding the pizza with one hand, she groaned and grabbed the offending device, squinting down at the caller ID.

Connor Randall?

Her confidential informant. The FBI considered him an asset. She considered him a pain in the neck. Right now, she sat in an unmarked car near the French Quarter, waiting to hear from him. He'd called her an hour earlier, stating that he'd been summoned by Louis Armond. The crime lord wanted to tell him something important. They were to meet at the opera house.

Please tell me this is all over and we finally have Armond. Josie's prayer filtered through her worry. She always prayed when she was on a stakeout. Tonight, she just prayed that Connor wouldn't do anything stupid.

"I hope you have good news," she said on a hopeful breath.

His slightly British accent tickled at her earlobe. "Gilbert, we've got a problem."

Well, that didn't take long. She'd only been paired as Randall's handler for a week or so, and that mostly meant keeping him alive or constantly questioning him about the Mafia boss he'd been shadowing for over a year now.

The Mafia boss who'd hinted at turning. Maybe tonight? He'd wanted to see Connor tonight. In his private booth at the opera. But only if Connor came alone and with no security or listening devices.

Josie's pulse moved too fast, causing her nerves to tighten like a twisted wire. "You're in trouble already?"

"Big trouble." He sounded breathless and not-so-cool-and-calm, that trace of an accent just barely detectable.

Trying to picture him untying the knot of his tuxedo tie, she focused on the here and now. "Did you kill someone?"

"No. But Armond's mistress is dead. He's with me and . . . he insisted I bring him out to Armond Gardens."

Insisted. Past tense. Connor was on the move. That meant she needed to be on the move right behind him.

Josie did a visual. The narrow side street glinted like a dark ribbon around shadows and shapes. No sign of anyone, though. Not even a stray cat. The opera house was a block away.

"Turn back, and we'll bring him into head-quarters." When Connor didn't respond, she said, "I don't have time for games, Randall."

"You can't bring either of us in. We're heading out of the city. And this is no game."

Dropping the pizza slice back into the small box on the seat, Josie sat up, her thoughts whirling. Maybe her new boss *didn't* like her, since from the minute she'd arrived at her new assignment, he'd teamed her up with the most notorious asset this division had ever encountered. Still wondering if that was a plus or a double negative, Josie figured babysitting a suave art thief turned informant must be punishment, pure and simple.

After a case gone bad in Dallas, she still carried a shield of guilt mixed with a solid need to find redemption, but Connor Randall was a live wire, not her ticket off the hot seat. Not redemption quality.

Connor Randall. Reformed con man now trying to save his own skin. Good-looking in a classic way with dark curly hair and rich blue eyes, he was comfortable in any situation and in any setting. The man moved so smoothly inside criminal circles it was hard to tell if he truly had turned toward the good side of the law. He had several aliases—Connor Simpson, Connor Clarence, Connor Butler. He could get in and out of the country like Houdini popping out of a water tank.

But he also knew how to escape just like Houdini.

Was he working with Armond to pull a fast one on her?

Okay, Josie, think. He's watched all the time. We can track him. No way he'd try to escape. No way he'd purposely be involved in a shooting. He'd go back to jail. Forever.

But he'd gone in without a wire or any trackers.

"Are you telling me the truth or—"

"I'm not playing you, Agent Gilbert. I need your help. And soon."

Josie held the phone between her left shoulder blade and her chin while she maneuvered her car out of the parking space. "Tell me everything. Now."

"Someone shot Louis Armond's mistress right in front of the opera house. I saw the whole thing and so did he, but . . . it came from the roof of a nearby building. A sniper with a silencer. Now *he* could be in danger. We need to hide him."

Josie almost laughed out loud. Hide Louis Armond? That was like trying to hide the statue of General Stonewall Jackson centered in the Square. Near impossible.

But if someone was onto them . . .

She'd read the file, knew the history. These two men both had a lot of enemies.

Randall's cover had almost been blown last year during the Benoit art heist involving Princess Lara Kincade but he'd managed to smooth that over enough to get back on the notorious Mafia lord's good side and work toward either turning him or bringing him to justice. He'd been seen out and about with Armond all over New Orleans. But Connor Randall wasn't the kind to sit around waiting. If the deal was off, they could both be on the run.

And this was a very big deal. Josie swallowed the bile of failure and glared at her phone. *Please, dear Lord, give me the strength and wisdom to get it right this time.*

Then she asked, "Are you kidding me?"

"Why would I kid about a thing like that? The man is in shock and he's pretty sure he's next. He even thinks the hit might have been meant for him." He went silent then added, "And if you can't do your job, I might be right there with him, since he's practically blackmailing me into helping him."

Josie wanted to say good riddance, but even though she'd been hardened by witnessing the worst kind of crimes imaginable, she hadn't resorted to letting people get killed on purpose. She'd become an agent after her father had been carted off to jail when she was a teenager. Her father, a con man who'd fooled everyone, even his own family, had masked his crimes behind the persona of a successful financial adviser and businessman.

No wonder she didn't trust Connor Randall.

She'd made up for the sins of her father by helping to bring in a couple of other most-wanted criminals. But then things had taken a bad turn.

She didn't like being glued at the hip to a man who represented everything she hated, but maybe that was the price she had to pay right now.

Since that art heist had also involved the infamous Mafia lord, everyone at the New Orleans division of the FBI had been on the alert. Connor Randall had been there that night in the dank, dark wine cellar of an old mansion in the Quarter. And he had shot and killed Frederick Cordello, the man who'd wanted the princess dead so he could take the priceless Benoit paintings he'd believed she had.

Ironically, Louis Armond, allegedly a millionaire con man himself who mostly dealt in fake designer purses and shoes and illegal sales of priceless art, had proof that the paintings belonged to him. But after the ensuing publicity and scandal behind the whole affair, Armond had decided to take the high road to stoke some of the heat. He'd sent the paintings off on a museum art tour and then he'd become a very important witness for the FBI. A reluctant secret witness who had yet to give them anything of significance.

"You need to come back to New Orleans," she said now, her gaze scanning the street behind her.

"No can do."

Anything could happen with Randall. Nice to look at but hard to read. She hadn't managed to get a bead on the real Connor Randall. Yet. But she couldn't leave him hanging. Armond wouldn't have any qualms about either shooting Connor or pinning the blame on him. Or worse, persuading Connor to turn. If he hadn't already.

She worked her own persuasion. "Louis Armond agreed to immunity in exchange for information, remember?"

"I took that into consideration when he scrambled into my car and held a gun on me. I can't come back to the city right now. Too hot. I found him . . . right after it happened, holding a weapon."

He lowered his voice. "Whoever did this sure scared the man. I'm his last hope and he's my only hope. If I don't help him cover this up, he'll kill me and be done with it."

"Well, that sure makes this more understandable," she said on a sarcastic note. Then she regretted that note. She'd learned not to take anything for granted, not even an informant who grated on her last nerve. Heading northwest out of town, she decided to play along. "Tell me what you need."

He let out an exasperated sigh. "Look, this is bad, but it's a chance to . . . get you inside his world."

Good point. That way, she could keep an eye on both of them and maybe convince Armond to cooperate.

"But what if this is a setup?" she asked, her mind moving through several scenarios. "Maybe he's luring you out so he *can* kill you. I mean, has he told you the big secret he wanted to share?"

"Not yet." She heard a chuckle. "As for him killing me, yes, he could do that. I've already considered that angle, but right now he's in no shape to kill anyone. He says he didn't kill his mistress and I believe him. I think a sniper made this hit. He thinks they're onto him and that they'll come after anyone associated with him, including me.

"He's so scared he might be willing to save us a lot of trouble by cutting an even better deal." He went silent for a second or two. "Armond isn't the kind to scare easily, so I'd say we're onto something big here. I just happened to be in the wrong place at the wrong time, and now I'm not at liberty to walk away."

Josie read between the lines. The man had him right where he wanted him. Connor could testify against Armond, and if he told the truth—that he'd seen the man holding a gun over a woman lying on the street—things could go bad for Armond. But if Connor could be persuaded to put a different spin on that story . . . well . . . he might get to live.

Right. She'd never known a Mafia boss to have a change of heart unless he thought there was something in it for him. This could get messy. Connor could turn back to the dark side to save his own hide.

"Where are you now?" she asked. She had the car out on the street, moving.

"We just arrived at his estate on the Old River Road. It's like a fortress, so he should be safe here for a while. I'm not sure how safe."

He gave her the address and some directions, but Josie was pretty sure this place wasn't on any map.

"Okay, got it. On my way."

"Oh, and by the way, we have to make him believe you will help us clean up this mess. If he asks, and trust me, he will, you have to be prepared to make this go away."

Connor ended the call before she had a chance to burst out laughing. Or protest.

Wondering why she hadn't become a teacher like her mother had suggested, Josie quickly called Special Agent in Charge Joseph Sherwood and explained what Connor had told her. "I'd like to go in alone and undercover for now, sir."

After a long silence, the older man said, "You can go in alone, but I'll have a team on standby in case you get into trouble. We've worked too hard to bring Armond in to let anything go wrong now."

There was another slight pause and then he added, "Meantime, let me know if you need any backstopping. I'll get the techs involved and I'll work with the locals on the shooting."

"Yes, sir." If he was willing to set up an undercover background for her, Sherwood must understand the magnitude of this mission. She might be in this for days, possibly weeks.

She'd go out to the Armond compound and get Armond and Connor to safety. That is, if someone else didn't beat her to the place and do harm to both of them.

TWO . . .

Josie checked her rearview mirror several times to make sure she wasn't being followed. Normal Saturday-night traffic streamed along the interstate.

She bumped up her speed, her pulse zooming along with the vehicle's high speed. Why was she so worried anyway? Connor could handle himself. He knew all the tricks of survival.

But . . . Connor Randall was almost legendary around the bureau, so maybe Armond considered him more valuable alive than dead right now. If anyone could charm a snake, it'd be Connor Randall. She didn't want to think about how he could turn a woman's head, too.

She hadn't decided if the debonair Mr. Randall had finally mended his ways or if he was just working on one last big con. They'd had several conversations, or as Connor liked to call them—interrogations. She asked questions, and he either answered with a cool disregard or said nothing at all. She'd pulled him in earlier today to get a better handle on tonight's mission, and the man had waltzed in wearing a custom-made tuxedo and a custom-made smile.

Get that out of your head, she told herself. So he was handsome and debonair and . . . still a criminal in her mind.

She only wanted to get Armond and him out alive and make sure Armond lived up to his side of this bargain. Her career needed a serious boost. If the Mafia lord was running scared, they'd never get the truth out of him.

Josie made a few turns to check any tails. She got off an exit ramp and looped back around to where she'd started, zooming as fast as she could.

There! She spotted another car behind her, doing the same loop. This time, she stayed on the interstate but zigzagged between other vehicles and took a different exit. When she felt sure she wasn't being followed, she exited again and took the back roads that followed the Mississippi River.

No other cars were in sight, so she breathed a sigh of relief. Whoever had been behind her was gone now.

Or maybe they were just waiting.

Connor might be right after all. Maybe this went deeper than just someone trying to take down Armond. Maybe someone was also after Connor. The list could be long and far-reaching. Which meant they might be watching her, too.

Located about forty-five minutes north of New Orleans and set back off a narrow country road near the Mississippi River, the Armond estate consisted of a stunning antebellum house that was well over one hundred and fifty years old and set in the middle of an acreage that rivaled Versailles.

Stately columns surrounded the big stucco house. Massive mushrooming live oaks that had been planted over three hundred years ago lined the long drive leading to the double front doors. A high black iron fence and electronic gate surrounded the whole thing, while armed guards and nasty watchdogs patrolled the perimeters.

Connor paced out on the downstairs gallery, walking from column to column while he waited for Josie Gilbert to arrive. A guard stood near the big double doors, making sure Connor didn't venture too far. Every now and then Connor would touch a hand to the still-warm eggshell-white patina of the old stucco. This house had good bones and an aged, distinguished history. When he'd first seen what was now called Armond Gardens, Connor thought this was exactly the kind of place he'd always dreamed of owning. But it hadn't taken him long to realize a mansion didn't make a home. A lot of criminal activities and nefarious comings and goings went on behind this tranquil, elegant facade. He didn't want to live here now. But he sure didn't want to die here, either. Not tonight.

Now he had a reason to live. He hoped to give his sister, Deidre, the kind of home she deserved even if he never lived there with her. His sister, just a few years younger than his thirty-two years, deserved a home of her own, and she deserved some peace of mind. He'd changed his ways for that purpose and he intended to see it through to prove to Deidre that he'd turned back toward the Lord.

His cell buzzed.

It was Armond, huddled up in the back of the house. "What is the holdup?"

"She's on her way," Connor said and then ended the call.

The man was seriously agitated, to the point of calling Connor himself rather than ordering a guard to carry a message. Someone had just murdered his young girlfriend, and he knew he might be next. Plus, he knew if his wife returned from New York and heard this, she'd leave him. Mrs. Armond had warned her philandering husband several times but Louis Armond thought he could get away with everything from murder to infidelity. Another great example of the criminal mind.

Somehow, he now expected—no, demanded—

Connor to fix this. Kind of ironic, considering Connor had a target on his back that had been put there because he'd been associating with Louis Armond. Was this payback time, or had Louis understood that Connor had witnessed part of the shooting and might be willing to tell all? Including the fact that Armond could have possibly been the shooter or hired the shooter. If Armond hadn't killed the woman, then who had? Connor wondered. And why had Armond been all alone on the street, without any of his guards?

Armond could have killed Connor several times over, tonight or any other night. They were out here away from the city in a fortress full of big-muscled bodyguards and a state-of-the-art security system. He'd be dead and buried in the river by now if Armond wanted him that way. The man knew Connor had worked with the FBI to take down Frederick Cordello for attempted art theft and murder. When Connor had shot Cordello to protect Princess Lara Kincade, Armond had witnessed the whole thing, but Connor had smoothed that one over by explaining the FBI had forced him to cooperate.

Which happened to be the truth.

That persuasive conversation, and Connor delivering on his promise to Armond, had saved Connor. For now. He'd found the famous Benoit paintings that technically and legitimately belonged to Armond. Armond already knew

Connor had no love for the FBI. If he played the hand he'd been given, Connor might be able to stay alive long enough to be free from both Armond and the FBI.

Finally.

Or he could be dead before morning.

"But you've got lawyers, people," Connor had reminded the man after Armond had jumped into his car and they'd hurried out of New Orleans. "I just happened to come along at the wrong time. I saw you standing there and I reacted."

"You were in the right place," Armond replied, a hint of fear coloring his nervous appreciation. "We have to keep this tight. No one can know I was associated with that poor girl. I can't call the lawyers or anyone else. Too dangerous." Then he'd turned in the seat, waving the weapon he still held. "You owe me, remember?"

So now Connor was being held as a "guest" in the Armond fortress. He'd wanted to get closer to the criminal, but not this way. Armond could turn trigger-happy and shoot him on the spot.

To keep building up to the rapport they'd once had, Connor asked the Mafia boss why he'd thought it a good idea to bring his girlfriend to the opera while his wife was out of town.

"She wasn't supposed to be there," Armond retorted. "I told her never to acknowledge me in public. But she showed up, scared and shouting at me to do something."

Armond thought he'd been set up by someone who wanted him dead. Someone who'd killed the girl just to show him they were serious. "I'll be next. That's how this works." He'd included Connor in his fears. "They know you were my close associate, so now they might know I'm in cahoots with the feds."

The scared bully had centered on Connor the way a newborn lamb might center on the human who'd fed him a bottle. Attachments such as this could only lead to more trouble. Connor was in so deep now, he wondered how he'd ever get out of this. But he could use this latest development to his advantage, at least.

Armond came out the door, sweating and ruddy-faced, surrounded by armed guards. "This woman—are you sure she can take care of this?"

Armond didn't know Josie. Up until a couple of weeks ago, Connor's handler had been a by-the-book veteran of the FBI. But John Burgess had abruptly decided to retire, and just like that, Josie Gilbert had walked into Connor's already-complicated life. That could work in their favor now, however. Armond technically didn't have any choice. He had to trust Josie, and he didn't have a clue that she was FBI.

"Yes," Connor replied, trying to piece things together, since he knew Josie would question him with a heavy-handed attitude. The newest FBI special agent to hit town did not approve of

Connor's methods. But they were stuck with each other until he could prove his merit and finally go free.

Right now, he had to get his facts straight regarding this bizarre turn of events.

The parking attendant had watched in surprise as Connor got back in his car and took off. He might have seen the whole thing, and by now the police and the FBI were probably swarming around the crime scene. The attendant could have given them Connor's license-plate number and a description of his car, too, but Sherwood obviously would already know Connor had been on the scene. Since the FBI kept tabs on his whereabouts, he understood they'd see him as a suspect. He had to have the story straight. And he was hoping Special Agent Josie Gilbert would agree with him on that.

"She's good, Louis. She has experience in these matters."

Or at least he hoped she did. If Josie would think beyond her distaste at having to work with Connor, she'd realize they had Armond. The man would do anything to stay out of the limelight and keep this nasty business from his irritable wife, or he could decide he no longer wanted to talk.

"Is she ever gonna get here?"

A car pulled around the curve and waited at the gate. Since Armond had already told security to let her in the minute she arrived, the gate swung open.

Connor's heartbeat slid into fast gear, the way it always did when he was on a big case. Or maybe tonight it was the added thrill of working with Josie Gilbert. Could he help it if he had a secret crush on her? He'd have to put all of that aside while they tidied up things. Now he had a niggling doubt regarding the newest addition to the New Orleans bureau. There was the Dallas incident that no one wanted to discuss.

"Go back inside, Mr. Armond," he suggested. "I'll update her and bring her to you."

Still dazed, Louis Armond nodded and hurried past two bodyguards into the big drawing room to the left of the central hallway. Connor nodded to one of the guards and shut the doors. He needed to prep Josie Gilbert.

Now the fun part. Had she trusted Connor enough to come alone? He prayed she'd been wise enough to know they had Armond cornered and scared. He also prayed they could use this little dustup to their advantage. If so, he might be able to finally shed Louis Armond's iron-tight grip and the halo of death that came with being in a forced alliance with a beautiful, determined female FBI agent.

That would, however, depend on how this night's work went, and whether he and Josie would live to see another day.

THREE . . .

Josie checked her gun and got out of the unmarked car, then took in her surroundings. The big antebellum house stood stately and quiet in the moonlight. It was beautiful, but tonight it held a sinister aura of death and destruction.

Nice digs, Mr. Armond. Sure that the original owners of this gracious old mansion would turn over in their graves at the sight of several armed guards with snarling dogs and three blacked-out luxury SUVs and the new name of Armond Gardens, she wondered exactly how much money it took to own such a showplace.

And how much of that money had been ill-gotten?

She ignored the shiver of unease that chased down her spine. She hadn't seen anyone following her since she'd left the main road, so she needed to relax and get on with this. But she had a bad feeling, a kind of fluttering in her stomach that indicated this whole setup felt wrong. Shaking it off, she did one more visual and prepared to get on with her work.

As she approached the wraparound porch, a man stepped out of the shadows, causing her to also wonder why she'd agreed to come out here to help someone she'd only met a few days ago. She was glad she'd reported her whereabouts back to the New Orleans bureau in spite of Connor telling her to keep quiet, and that she'd warned Sherwood that things might get dicey.

"Bring him in, Gilbert. Nothing dicey about that."

Did he mean Louis Armond or Connor Randall? Sherwood didn't care for the charming informant. But Joseph Sherwood didn't seem to care for anyone around him, for that matter.

"Sir, I can't do that." She explained on the way out what Connor had told her. "Armond refuses to let him leave. So he's set me up to help with the situation. Alone. Armond doesn't want the feds anywhere around this estate. Let me go in and see what I can find. Randall and I will figure out how to handle this, and I'll try to keep you posted. But I need your permission to go dark if necessary."

Sherwood had reluctantly agreed. Now she had to show him she knew her stuff. Her boss already gave off an air of disdain whenever she spoke to him. Maybe he resented having to take on an agent who'd messed things up in her last assignment.

Just one more reason for Josie to make this one work.

Connor Randall met her at the low steps onto

the brick-floored porch. Glancing toward the two-ton guard at the door, he pulled Josie aside. "You did come alone, right?"

She wanted to say, *"No, actually, I brought the whole New Orleans bureau with me."* But she was too intrigued and too hopeful that she could corner two rats at once. Tonight's operation had her rattled. She was out here on her own, with no backup, making this up as she went. She wouldn't admit that part of the shake-up inside her soul had to do with this man, who sure looked good in a tux.

"I'm alone," she replied. Then she lowered her voice. "But I did report in, since my SAC told me to bring you both back to town, so I can't hold them off for too long. The news of a dead woman near the opera house has already hit the airwaves."

She didn't need to explain that the FBI and the NOPD already had forensic teams on-site at the crime scene. The locals would take the lead, then turn things over to the FBI.

Connor's expression turned dark and hard to read. "Has Armond's name come up?"

"Not yet to the public. But I'm to get you both to a safe house immediately."

Connor's surprised look changed to a resolved one. "And you managed to hold Sherwood off for a while?"

"Yes, but he wasn't happy. He wants to go

by the book on this one so Armond won't bolt."

"Any mention of a black sports car on the scene?"

She shook her head. "Only a dark car. That's the official word." Tired of the interrogation, she said, "I need to be briefed, and don't leave anything out."

"I'll explain everything," he said.

"You'd better. I'm risking a lot, coming here on my own."

Too late, she realized she was also locked in. The high iron fences and the army of guards told the tale of illegal comings and goings. What if Armond refused to let either of them leave? She'd read dossiers about torture tactics and worse, especially regarding agents who'd been caught. And she knew firsthand what could happen to informants who got caught. Putting those images out of her mind, Josie gathered her thoughts.

"Armond might pretend to be ready to cooperate, but someone scared him silly tonight. He's desperate and that can be dangerous." The threat of death made people do desperate things.

Connor cleared his throat and whispered close, "But we've got him right where we want him. He believes you're here to help us. And . . . he's kind of holding this over my head, if you get my drift."

"How did you get involved, anyway?" she asked while she did another visual of the well-lit gardens and the too-dark tree line. Even with guard dogs, someone with criminal intent could get in here. "He and you should have been inside, finishing up with what we hope is the information we've all been waiting for."

"I was on my way in when this happened. I'd just turned into the parking garage." He glanced back at the double front doors. "I saw Armond standing there with his mistress. Which was so not like Armond. Then I saw the woman fall to the ground. I backed out of the garage and floored it to Armond. He was leaning over her in shock, a gun in his hand."

"You saw him shoot her?"

"No. I saw him leaning over her with a gun. But when he looked around and glanced up to the rooftop above them, I figured a sniper had done it."

"So you stopped to chat?"

"I stopped and called out to him to get in my car. His guards hurried to surround him, but he turned and came around my car and jumped inside. Told me to drive."

"Why did you take that chance?" she asked, wondering if he'd thought this through. "You should have called me right away."

"He seemed especially grateful to have a getaway car, and his guards scattered, so I had to do something. Then he held a gun to my head," Connor replied. He shrugged as if this whole affair was nothing much. "Two thoughts entered my mind. One, he wanted me to get him out of there, and two, he was so erratic, he might decide to shoot me if I didn't do his bidding."

Ignoring his cool explanation, she asked, "And you didn't think to call this in to 911?"

"Look, I've been tailing him when I could. I know I'm supposed to stay out of sight but I was so close to getting him for good last year. And tonight, well, I thought this would finally be over. This was supposed to be the last time I had to deal with the man."

He put a hand against one of the colossal columns and gave her a blue-eyed stare. "I didn't think. I just went after him before he got shot, too. If he gets himself killed, we'll never get the information and evidence we need to get to the real power behind his empire."

"Great. So now I'm an unofficial accomplice to two of my informants leaving the scene of a murder?"

"He didn't kill her," Connor replied. "He was with her, but he didn't kill her. The kill shot hit her clean and right between the eyes, and I didn't hear the shot. That means it came from a distance and it was silenced. He did pull out his gun, so someone could have seen that and misinterpreted it."

She doubted him already. She wasn't confident in the plan to come out here, since Connor had been the one to mastermind it. Josie liked to be in control, so her first few weeks on the job at her new assignment were not going as she'd planned. She couldn't afford to mess up another big case with a wanted suspect. And yet, she'd gone way beyond the call of duty by convincing her boss that she needed to see this through. Now, why was that?

Maybe it had been the hard-edged request from Connor over the phone, or it could now be the serious glint in Connor's storm-blue eyes. Why did they seem so much darker in the moonlight? And why in the world should she trust this man?

Well, the higher-ups—excluding Sherwood, of course—seemed to dote on him and praised his services, assuring her that Connor Randall had turned over a new leaf. Since she didn't always believe in second chances or quick change-of-heart turnovers, she found that hard to swallow. She was about to test that theory.

Could she be sure? *Lord, grant me wisdom.*

"What do you expect me to do, besides haul you both in?"

Connor gave her that steady, level stare that worked on most other women. "I expect you to do your job. We have one of the most notorious mobsters in this country in there waiting for us to help him out of a sticky situation. And we don't have much of a choice, the way I see it." He leaned close, his smile as enticing as the moonlight. "And we could both use a break, don't you think?"

Josie pushed at her hair, rattled that he knew her history about as well as she knew his. Okay, so they both had trust issues. And the need to clear a few bad marks. "Yeah, there is that."

He must have sensed her doubts. "Look, I appreciate this. You're with me. You're safe."

"I don't need you to keep me safe," she retorted, touching the gun strapped to her belt. Her whisper was for his ears only. "I'm a big girl, Mr. Randall. I was top of my class at Quantico."

He held her arm. "Before we go in there, you need to understand something. Being top of your class at anything doesn't matter to these people. They are the worst kind of scum, and they would sooner butcher you than look at you."

Blood-soaked images flashed through her head. She'd been undercover during a drug raid in Dallas and . . . she'd messed up big-time. Her informant, a young female recovering junkie, had been tortured and left for dead because of one slipup. Josie's slipup. She couldn't let bad information be her guide ever again.

Somewhere off in the bug-infested woods, an owl hooted. Then she heard the flutter of powerful wings.

Another shiver of apprehension went down Josie's spine, but she shook it off. "Got it. I'm good." She stared over at him, took a breath. "I'll do whatever it takes to bring this man down. If we help him tonight, we'll have leverage, and hopefully, that will convince him to give us the goods on his operation."

"Exactly," Connor said as he ushered her to the big front doors. "He hasn't executed me yet because I'm the only witness and my testimony can save him. And he's kind of blackmailing me into helping to save his hide. See, we do think alike."

"For now," she replied, thinking a jury wouldn't trust either the Mafia don or the good-looking man in the tux. She sure didn't, now that he'd told her he *was* doing this to save himself. What a noble concept. "But, Randall . . . don't take me for granted, ever."

"Wouldn't dream of it."

Once they were inside, the elegant warmth of the old mansion shimmered in hues of tasteful art, glittering crystal and aged bone china. The place looked untouched, like something out of another century. But the creepy factor echoed in the garish glowing yellow lights and the scent of too much aftershave.

"Swag," she whispered to Connor. "By the way, let's start with first names only unless I have to tell him I'm also FBI."

It still smarted that her new supervisor had kept her so out of the loop on a lot of things regarding

Louis Armond that she'd been forced to tug information out of Connor instead. She was surprised Sherwood had let her take point on a one-woman stakeout tonight. But Sherwood had warned her he'd also have a team of other agents out and about, too.

Fat lot of good that had done Armond.

Before he could respond, two big men came up the hall. "We need to check for wires or weapons," one of them growled.

"I have one gun," Josie offered, lifting her jacket to show her weapon. "And if you expect me to help with this little problem, I'm keeping it."

Connor gave a slight nod to the men. After patting her down and checking the gun, they seemed satisfied. But they also followed on her heels.

He turned her to the left and motioned her inside the big, antique-filled drawing room, then closed the aged pocket doors. "Mr. Armond, this is my friend . . . Josie."

"Does your friend Josie have a last name?" Armond asked, clearly in control of himself now that help had arrived.

"Just Josie for now," she replied before Connor could come up with a name. "You only need to remember that."

"I see, Just Josie."

Armond sat in a brocade high-backed antique

chair, a cup of coffee steaming on the table beside him. His salt-and-pepper hair was crisp with some sort of pomade but his olive-colored skin was pale against his white tuxedo shirt. Did everyone around here wear tuxedos?

Armond gave her a thorough once-over. "So, Connor has briefed you on the situation and . . . you can take care of this?"

Ah, there was that bit of fear and doubt she'd expected. "Yes, he did, and I can, sir. The good news is that no one has come forward stating they saw you with the girl. So far Connor is your only witness and he can vouch for you. The bad news is that, yes, she's dead and, yes, the NOPD is all over this."

"So my name hasn't come up?"

"Not so far. The only news right now is that there's been a shooting near the Quarter." She pulled out her cell. "I'm checking any trending right now."

"Trending?" Armond looked confused.

Connor stepped forward. "Why don't we sit down?"

Josie sat beside him on an exquisite butter-yellow brocade sofa. "Trending—it means news of your mishap might be all over the internet or evening news by now. We'll check for any witnesses, any mentions of your name, any videos streaming about a woman being murdered."

Armond's face twisted. "Lewanna. That's the

woman." Then he changed his tune. "Isn't that dangerous, checking on your phone?"

She shook her head. "It's a burner."

"Of course," Connor said on a reassuring note. "I told you Josie knows her stuff."

Armond didn't look convinced. "So . . . what should I do now?"

"I'd say we wait," Josie replied, her fingers tapping on her phone. It really was a burner. She'd hidden her secure work cell in her car, where his men couldn't find it when they went out to do a search. She'd fill the burner with what she needed and send it to the fake email account she used as Josie Grant. Then she'd hide the phone in her lockbox in her apartment. If she got out of here alive, of course.

"Look, Mr. Armond, your girlfriend got shot on a city street and there's bound to be other witnesses who will come forward and tell what they saw." She leaned forward, her dark bangs covering her face in what she hoped was an intimidating, mysterious way. "Some of them could lie, so it's a good thing Connor came along when he did. He knows the truth."

Glancing over at Connor, she caught a whiff of admiration before his eyes went dark again. Then she turned back to Armond and did her tough-girl act. "Did you see the shooter?"

Armond shook his head. "No. I was too busy telling Lewanna to leave. We could never be seen together." He held his hand to his head as if he had a bad headache. "I can't believe she's dead. If my wife hears this . . ."

Connor got up and poured coffee for Josie and then got himself a cup. "So why did she show up at the opera?"

"She was frightened," Armond replied, his hand shaking when he tried to take a sip from his cup. He finally gave up and grabbed a silver flask off the table. Opening it, he poured what looked like whiskey into his coffee. "I've never seen Lewanna like that. Someone had left a nasty note on her porch, along with a dead rat."

"Do you think she ratted someone out?" Josie asked.

"No, but someone thinks she did. And that means they also think I ratted them out. Lewanna showed me the note."

Connor glanced over at Josie and then turned back to Armond. "Do you have that note?"

Armond looked shocked, as if he'd forgotten. "I tucked it into my pocket." He pulled the crushed paper out and stared down at it, then began reading.

"Your boyfriend has been playing outside the boundaries. Tell Armond he's a dead man if he crosses that line again."

He threw the letter down and stared at Connor. "They know something. They musta found out I was meeting you tonight to give you information."

"You can still give us information," Connor replied, his gaze full of resolve.

"Did you read that note?" Armond asked in a shout.

Josie took her napkin and reached for the paper, careful to keep her fingerprints off it. "Cutouts from magazines. How juvenile."

"How serious," Armond replied. "It might look like I killed her, but I didn't. I was standing there trying to talk her into leaving. I had dismissed my guards for the sake of privacy." He rubbed a hand down the bald spot on top of his head. "Happened so fast. Had to be a sniper. It's a terrible thing, her being shot. But I'm a target, and someone wants me to be aware of that."

He finished his spiked coffee, back to being the boss he thought he was. "I need you two to get to the bottom of this. Right away. And you need to tell the feds all deals are off."

Connor gave Josie another glance. "You don't trust your own people, so that means you think this is an inside job?"

Armond nodded, shrugged. "I've made many enemies. Some of my close associates have betrayed me." His keen stare indicated that Connor was one of those.

Josie did an eye lift to show her displeasure. "Let's start at the beginning," she said. "We'll need a list of anyone you might have inadvertently offended, especially recently. And we need to check all your personal weapons to see if anything is missing." She tapped notes into her phone.

"Maybe they made it seem like a sniper, but someone else with a closer aim could have done it with a different weapon and a silencer." She tapped notes into her phone. "The forensic team and medical examiner can determine that if they can find any bullets to compare. Based on the angle and where the bullet entered, the type of weapon, all of that will come into play."

"The shot could have come from the building directly right behind us." Armond nodded, snapped his fingers to bring a guard running. After he'd ordered sandwiches, paper and pen, he turned back to Josie and Connor. "You'll stay here at Armond Gardens as my guests while you're doing the legwork, understand."

"That wasn't a question," Connor said low to Josie.

"Connor is a very smart man," Armond said, his demeanor calm now. "He owes me his life, and right now, the only thing keeping him and you alive is my need for expediency on this pressing matter. Do you understand what I'm saying, Josie?"

"Clear as a bell, Mr. Armond. We're going on a

quest of sorts. If we succeed, we live. If we don't, we die. Am I right?"

Armond's chuckle was low and sure. "I like this woman."

She understood the command. Giving Connor a frustrated glare, she turned back to the man sitting like a king across from them. "Okay, then. We'll start with your immediate staff and work our way out. And I can promise you both, I'll take care of whoever is behind this."

And you, too. She would definitely take care of business with Louis Armond. But right now, she was playing a dangerous game. She wasn't sure if she could help convince Armond to seek immunity and protective custody or try to save him from someone even more dangerous. But Josie did know she had to make sure she kept herself and Connor alive, because they had one thing in common. They both wanted this man out of commission.

FOUR . . .

Armond had left them alone, but a member of his security team stood just outside the partially opened pocket doors. He'd been so paranoid, he'd rushed out of the room with his guard, but he'd ordered a giant named Beaux to guard the door.

Josie had no doubt that Armond would attempt to monitor their conversation. As paranoid as he seemed, he'd have set up security measures in every room in this sprawling mansion.

She went around the big room, touching things here and there in search of electronic bugs. When she was satisfied they were clear, she stared over at Connor and started whispering. "Look, I can't just hang out here with you and Armond. I'm sure a team is already in place to get to the bottom of this, and they'll want an update."

Connor stepped close. "Careful. That priceless bust on the table by the window has its eye on us."

Josie tipped her chin in acknowledgment. "Thanks for the heads-up. But we still need to discuss how we're to handle this."

Connor let her go, then paced back and forth in front of the fireplace. "Even though I vouched for you, they won't leave us alone for very long, so we need to compare notes. I've stayed here before, so I know it's not easy to get out. They'll make sure we can't leave if they don't want us to leave."

"Why? What good is there for Armond to hold us?"

"None, unless he thinks he needs us for leverage or bargaining. But he's a hands-on kind of criminal. He'll want to hover nearby until we prove to him we can help him. We have to convince him that he's not in danger and that we're on the level with him. If not, he'll be done with us and . . . we'll disappear in a permanent way."

"Which is why I had to inform my superior," she reminded him. "I'm already pushing it by being here without backup."

"I can try to get us out of here if things get ugly," Connor replied, still whispering. "I know all the secret passages, but the security here is ironclad."

Of course he knew all the secret passages. "That's why he's keeping you so close," she offered. "He's afraid you'll squeal."

"I don't kiss and tell," Connor said, his eyes hitting on her lips. "I was close to ending this last year, but that art-heist fiasco kind of blew that out of the water. This is a second chance, if you look at being held captive as a positive thing."

"A risky chance," she replied. Josie tried to reestablish her position. "I get that you're part of the inner circle, but I do have a job to do, remember? I can't hang out and pretend I'm some mysterious cleaner. Armond expects action, not explanations."

He shot a covert glance toward the hallway. "I can do the talking for both of us. Leave you out of any threads."

What, did the man use a messenger pigeon? "I'm already tangled up in all the threads," she retorted. "Besides, I have a secure phone in my car."

"And how do you propose we get to that phone?"

Josie couldn't believe she'd walked into such a convenient trap. "You've got me right where you want me, Randall. What's the deal here?"

His face tightened into an irritated glare. "The deal is—I asked for your help and you came. So we have to see this through. Get over the notion that I'm out to do you in. I have enough problems without that kind of attitude."

The man who'd fooled so many people was lecturing her about attitude? Josie wanted to handcuff him and take him into town, fast. But she had agreed to help him. Getting Armond had to be her only goal. For now.

"Okay, so what's the protocol? How did you handle things with your last liaison?"

Connor lowered his voice again. "I came and went on my own most of the time, but when I needed to get a message out, I sent a text on a secure phone to an address that looks like it belongs to my sister, Deidre." He put a finger to his lips to indicate they still needed to whisper.

Josie mouthed the words. "With an encryption?" How cloak-and-dagger of him.

"Yes, several codes. My *friends* know all of them." He touched on his phone.

Josie nodded. The text messages were rerouted to the FBI. "I see your point."

"Will that work?"

She nodded. "We need to let my, uh . . . boss know I'll be late for work." She glanced around, sure someone was listening right along with watching them. "Really late."

"I'll fix it," he replied.

Not liking his smug tone, she shook her head. "No, *we'll* fix it. You don't make a move without me, understand?"

"Got it." But he gave her a look that indicated he didn't like her bossing him around. Then he started back tapping at his phone.

Wanting to wipe that smug smirk off his handsome face, she got right in his ear. "Maybe your last contact got transferred for this very reason, Randall. You didn't play by the rules, and you didn't bring Armond down when you had a chance."

His expression hardened to stone. "Look, we can play this game of 'I don't like you, Connor Randall' all night or we can get word out that you're in and we're a team now."

He was right. They were wasting time standing here while Armond could be escaping out the back door. Or worse, while he waited for them to force the issue, or else. "If his people do a background search, they might figure out I'm FBI," she said. "So we need to establish that I'm legit so we can stall him. Once we have him at the safe house, I'll come clean."

Connor clicked his phone. "I'll tell Deidre that I can't wait to see her on Mother's Day."

"That's sweet, but this doesn't involve your mother."

"If you studied my file, you'd know my mother is dead," he retorted with iron force.

"Sorry," Josie replied, truly apologetic. She had studied his file. Several times. She should have remembered that fact, but the man had her all tied in knots. She attributed that to plain not liking him and missing her favorite pizza, but she had a feeling it went deeper than that. "Mother's Day is your code . . . for what?"

"Mother's Day means I'm in," he explained. "My fail-safe is Thanksgiving."

Josie almost smiled at that. "Is the Easter Bunny one of your cute little codes?"

"Funny." He didn't laugh. "No, but Memorial Day is coming up. A whole month or so with you, *Josie*. I see fireworks in my future and, yes, this could be memorable."

"Just get back on task," she replied, but she saw the gleam in his interesting eyes. So Mr. Cool had a sense of humor and he knew how to flirt. Too bad she really didn't care. "So we go with Mother's Day. And?"

"And I'll be staying here for the weekend with my friend Josie, who needs to settle in and get established in her new position. Josie 'handles' things for people."

"All right. We should be okay for now. But I do want to check on the latest update." She didn't like putting the cart before the horse, but what else could she do? They were stuck here with Armond until they could produce a plan of action.

So they both went to work, sending cryptic messages and waiting for even more cryptic replies. Soon they had enough of an update to give Armond a fresh report.

"We could tell him the truth," she suggested on a read-my-lips whisper, her mind whirling.

"Excuse me?"

If this hadn't been so serious, she would have laughed at the comical shock on his face. "We tell him it's been handled. Which it has. We can inform him we've called our contacts and he's safe as long as he does exactly what we tell him to do." She started tapping away on her burner again. "I'll even call some of my other confidential informants to make sure we have the right information."

"And?"

"And we show him why we need to focus on keeping him safe. We can't go after whoever did this if we're babysitting a paranoid Mafia boss. We need to move him to another location."

Connor relaxed again. "That's a good point. If the locals and the FBI can keep his name out of this for now, we can search for the real killer, and if we find that person, we'll have them both in a corner." He glanced toward the door. "And an added bonus—we get to live."

Josie crossed her arms. "Armond has to trust us with sensitive information, so we need to really make this work."

"I can handle him," Connor replied. "He'll come around if I keep working on him."

She saw the confidence in his eyes. "You sure are smug for someone who walks in two worlds. You expect the man who probably wants you dead to trust you?"

"I'm trying to be low-key and relaxed for the camera." He moved close. "So far, we've been whispering, but maybe we should act a little more lovey-dovey for the tiny red button embedded in that beautiful woman's necklace."

She didn't dare turn to look at the stone-faced interpretation of a woman draped in robes. The one he'd mentioned earlier. But she scratched her ear and mouthed *I don't see how being lovey-dovey can help us.*

He flashed his classic charmer smile. "I don't know. Just smile and pretend you like me, and who knows, maybe you will one day."

She grimaced and then laughed. "Too late for that. Why don't we continue to pretend we're putting our heads together to figure this out?"

"We are doing that." He tipped his forehead to

hers, then stood back. "I like literal interpretations."

Shocked at how much that brief contact had zapped her awareness, she asked, "Is that your secret-handshake kind of thing?"

"That's my staying-alive kind of thing. I have to be a carefree drifter who has a new woman on his arm every night. You need to be my latest conquest."

Josie didn't want to think about that, and she didn't want to acknowledge the hum of curiosity and chemistry his words provoked. Now was not a good time to explore that little tug she'd felt earlier. "Don't count me in on that list."

"I wouldn't dream of doing that. Not in reality. Right now, however . . ."

"We pretend."

"Yes. Hard as that might be for you, we need to ramp up the sizzle that Armond will expect. If he thinks we're close, he'll be distracted, and that will crack his famous armor."

Josie conceded yet again but her heart shouted a warning. Connor's explanation was so smooth she felt the kiss of silk moving over her skin. She was supposed to be professional and courteous while she gave Armond a show? "The sizzle? Like bacon on a hot griddle?"

"Exactly." His eyes lit up into a shimmering blue-gray as he turned and tapped out a text report. "We might end up liking each other yet."

"Don't get your hopes up on that," she retorted. But she still felt the warm imprint of his touch after she said it.

Connor paced, his mind clicking with ideas. He was used to taking care of himself, but now he had Josie to think about. True, she was a trained agent, but his last FBI handler had been a tall, strapping fiftysomething family man. Big difference.

Of course, Josie Gilbert would tell him to drop the protective-male persona. She gave off so many hostile vibes he was surprised he hadn't been burned by electricity by now.

Just one more thing for him to deal with—a bitter female FBI agent. Bitter? Or just determined to prove her worth after that little dustup in Dallas?

Connor certainly could understand that concept, since his now-dead mother had been a hard-core, bitter working woman. He didn't mind that so much, but being around Josie only made him want things he couldn't have. He'd been on his own for too long now to think about normal, mundane things such as dating or dancing or settling down. He would never admit it, but he liked working with the feds on the good side of the law. For a change. He did the same things that he'd always done, but now he used his experience and talent to help bring in criminals.

That gave him a bit of redemption, at least.

He wondered about Josie. What drove her to be so structured and buttoned-up? Had she believed she'd come from a normal, peaceful family or had she known early on that something was off with her successful father? Had she grown up in a small town with the white picket fence and the whole cheerleader, high-school-prom persona? Probably. Until it had all come crashing down.

That crash and burn would explain her need for justice now.

He'd have to find out so he could see inside her head. Sure, he'd found her file and . . . studied it, but some of the things that had transpired in Dallas were on a need-to-know basis. Probably to protect her identity. Connor wanted the real Josie to show up.

But right now, Louis Armond was waiting in his office for an update. So Connor planned to give him one.

"Are you ready?" he asked Josie.

"Ready, set, go," she retorted on a close whisper. "We've covered every angle, including a thorough email report to Sherwood. If Armond asks for my credentials, we give him a rundown. If that doesn't work, we give him the phone number."

"And he'll call and get a glowing report on your services."

"Everything is in place," she whispered. "We're

51

on our own unless we give the fail-safe signal." She adjusted her black leather jacket. "And I'm not talking Mother's Day here, Randall."

"Why don't you call me Connor?" he suggested, hoping to crack just a tiny edge of that chip on her shoulder.

"Why don't you just lead on?" she replied.

But he did see a trace of acceptance in her eyes. Progress, at least.

"All right, so we have our stories straight?"

She gave him a curt nod.

Connor turned to the giant guard waiting outside the drawing-room doors. He prayed this would work and that Armond would finally agree to immunity in exchange for his testimony regarding his nefarious associates. Connor had managed to unearth enough information to know the man had some sort of silent partner.

"Let's get this show on the road," he said to Josie.

She gave him a look of resolve and challenge.

Josie Gilbert might be the biggest challenge he faced right now.

FIVE . . .

The giant took them to the back of the house, where Armond's massive study offered a wall of windows that gave a stunning view of the back gardens. With moonlight and strategically placed spotlights shining on it, the big sloping yard took on an ethereal glow. Only, tonight the moonlight seemed to chase after too many shifting shadows. Was someone out there right now, ready to do harm to all of them?

Josie's golden-green eyes widened with a grudging admiration of the view, but she wiped her expression clean and turned tough again. "Mr. Armond, we've talked to all of our sources, and so far, you're in the clear. No new information. But the police do know Lewanna's identity, and they do have witnesses that reported seeing a man holding a gun standing near the body. Since the shot was muffled with a silencer, no one heard anything." That had just come via rerouted text straight from her supervisor.

She tossed things over to Connor with a solemn stare.

"No one has yet identified me or my car," Connor said. "If anyone saw you get in my car, they're not talking."

"Any reports of other such shootings?" Armond asked, clearly still shaken.

"No," Connor replied. "Do you expect that?"

"I have no idea," Armond retorted. "But if they were willing to kill Lewanna, they'll probably try to kill anyone else close to me." He glanced out the window, then back at Connor. "You already know too much. Some of my associates might feel the same way now." He shook that off with a shrug. "I'm glad my wife is safe in New York."

"Are you sure she's safe?" Josie asked, her tone as warm and unaffected as the still wind outside.

"I have people in place," Armond said with another shrug.

"Can you trust them?" Connor asked, wondering why Armond didn't trust his local security team.

"I have to trust them right now," Armond responded. "I'm a sitting duck. I knew better than to get involved with the feds. Starting with you."

"You *can* trust me," Connor replied, hating the lie but using his close relationship with the old man as collateral.

"I only need you now to hide me and help keep me safe," Armond retorted. "Don't make me regret that decision."

And so much for that. Connor glanced at Josie. "He's right. We have to be careful here. A lot of unsavory people know I work for Mr. Armond."

Armond's bushy brows lifted at that statement.

"You used to work for me, but we both know why I had to . . . let you go."

Connor cleared his throat. "Yes, but I'm back for now. If everyone can work with that?"

"I don't have a choice and you certainly don't," Armond said, his gaze saying otherwise. "But I'm watching you, Randall." He gave Josie a harsh appraisal. "And I'm still not sure about you, young lady. I'll have my people do a rundown on you, but I need your full name."

Josie gave him one of her undercover names. "Grant. Josie Grant."

"Do you mind if I do a background check?"

"Not a problem for me," Josie replied, her tough-girl stance sounding completely real. She tossed her straight dark hair and crossed her arms over her shiny black leather jacket. "I always watch my back." She tapped her phone. "*I've* put people in place to squelch any rumors. And I've already done my homework on you. Your name won't cross any lips." Her eyes slanted up. "You command a lot of respect around these parts, Mr. Armond."

Armond chuckled. "And I intend to keep it that way." But he didn't sound so confident right now. After giving her name to one of the guards, he waited, staring at them until the man returned and whispered something in his ear.

"Seems you also command a great deal of respect, Josie . . . Grant."

"That's what I get paid for," Josie replied, obviously relieved that Sherwood and the techs had managed to set up a cover so quickly. She named her price and waited. Armond's slight nod got his men moving. Josie sent the old man a lifted eyebrow in thanks.

Nerves of steel, Connor decided. He liked that in a woman.

Connor wondered if Armond truly did care about his wife or his grown son. The man was all about making more money, and he really didn't care how he did that. Or who he hurt or destroyed in doing it. But he'd made and lost more money than anyone knew, and he'd had to get into cahoots with some ruthless people. In return, he'd pledged to keep names out of the conversation. Until the FBI had cornered him and offered him a deal he couldn't refuse. No wonder he was afraid someone was after him. They'd need to remember that, too.

"Did you make that list of people you suspect?" Josie asked. "I can get right on that, since we've done a rundown on any chatter and cleaned that up for now." She glanced around the room. "And we need to check your personal weapons."

"I have the list you requested but it's only a partial one."

Connor's hope deflated. The man still refused to name the main players. Witnessing the death of his mistress had done exactly what those players wanted it to do—scare Armond back into silence.

"Let's get started on checking the weapons," Josie said, shifting a worried glance toward Connor.

Armond motioned to a guard to open the weapons cabinet on the other side of the room. "And call down and have someone check all of the weapons in the cellar cabinet, too." After a few minutes of waiting silence, Armond held up the list, but kept it away from Josie. "Just how exactly do you expect to continue cleaning up this situation?"

Connor had expected this. Armond didn't trust anyone, but then he was a powerful man with a lot of powerful rivals. He'd go for nothing less than an all-out protection detail.

Before Josie could reply, a guard came in and whispered into Armond's ear again. Armond's almond-colored eyes widened.

"One of my high-powered rifles is missing."

Josie turned to the guard to jot down the make and model of the missing weapon. Then she put her hands down on Armond's desk. "That means even if you didn't pull the trigger, someone took one of your weapons to make it look like you ordered the hit."

"I bought that particular rifle for . . . my son."

Connor grunted. "If they find one of your guns near the crime scene, you can bet they'll want to question you."

"I thought you were taking care of things," Armond blurted, his anger boiling over toward Josie.

Josie went into tough-chick mode with a flip of those long, tattered brunette bangs. "Hey, I've already had a thorough report of the crime scene, and they didn't find a gun. And we both patched things up to make sure your name won't come up for now." She put her hands on her hips and walked straight to the end of Armond's huge teakwood desk. "I didn't come out here in the middle of the night to enjoy the view, Mr. Armond. I'm good at what I do, but if you wanna find someone else—"

"I don't," he said, waving a hand to a hovering guard. "I just have to be sure about these things."

"We all have to be sure," Connor said, stepping in. "You need to get out of here. Josie and I think we need to go back into the city to do some footwork."

"Unacceptable. I have the latest electronic equipment right here. You can research anything you need."

Josie hit a palm on the desk. "Look, Mr. Armond, I know who you are and what you do. That's not my problem. But if you want my services, then first, you need to pay me my asking price, and second, you need to trust me completely. Stop playing this game of passive-aggressive control. I'll go out that door right now and leave you and your men here to finish this job."

"You leave when I say so," Armond retorted.

"You're not my boss," Josie replied.

Connor smelled a fight. Maybe Josie was spoiling for one, but he wasn't. Not just yet.

"Hey, we have to stick together," he said on an easy breath. "You don't trust me, but remember, I did help you find the Benoit paintings—all three of them. And I haven't sold you out to the FBI even though they've pulled me in, several times."

He glanced at Josie, remembering how she'd been in on one of the last debriefings he'd had to endure. "I'm here to help, Mr. Armond. You can still make a clean break by telling us who your partner is. Or haven't you realized that someone inside your organization is betraying you in a big way?"

"And that person could easily be you," Armond replied.

"Me?" Connor held up his hands. "I don't like guns. And why would I take out Lewanna? She seemed like a nice girl."

"You shut up about Lewanna," Armond shouted with a finger in Connor's face. "You're here because I decided to use your expertise instead of wasting you or maybe *before* I waste you," Armond reminded him. "Just remember that whenever you think about walking away."

"Nobody's walking here," Josie replied, her

eyes snapping with annoyance. "We're here to protect you, and it seems apparent that someone close to you is involved in this. Let's get over the paranoia and work on getting to the bottom of this."

Armond stared up at her, his dark brown eyes burning between insolence and fear. Josie stared right back, her expression unrelenting.

Armond finally sat back in his big leather chair. "What happens next?"

Josie stood, gave Connor a relieved glance and then turned back to Louis Armond. "We make a plan to move you. But until then, you stay put with your guards. You don't let anyone but the two of us in or out of this compound."

"Understood."

Connor took over. "We go into the city, do our thing with setting you up in a safe place. Look for that missing gun. We'll question the kind of people the police can't even begin to find and we'll get to the truth about who killed Lewanna."

"You will report back to me."

Not a question, but a demand.

"Of course." Connor came to stand by Josie. "I'll keep you posted."

Armond stood and shook his head. "I need a more reassuring guarantee. Before I agree to move, you have to agree to one of my men accompanying you at all times. As insurance, of course."

Josie let out a sigh. "You need to trust us."

Armond motioned for the giant. "I will, because Beaux is going to be with you. He knows how to make people more trustworthy."

Connor and Josie exchanged looks. Beaux was big, really big, and he had a perpetual scowl on his meaty face. He'd be hard to shake. And deadweight in quick getaways.

"Uh, that's not such a good idea, Mr. Armond," Connor replied.

"Then we all sit here and watch and wait," Armond retorted.

Josie let out an exaggerated grunt. "Look, let's just get moving with this before someone comes after you again. If he wants to tag along, then so be it. I refuse to sit here wasting precious time when I could be out there clearing you of any wrongdoing."

She gave Connor a look that could have melted the Remington sculpture displayed behind Armond's desk. This was not going to be easy. But then, Connor had learned that working with criminals and agents never was. And here he stood caught between two very opposing forces.

He had a feeling things would only get worse.

Things got worse in the next second.

They heard an explosion somewhere deep in the interior of the house.

SIX . . .

Armond's guard jumped to his aid and pushed him down behind the big desk and shouted, "He's okay. But we need to get him out of here."

Connor grabbed Josie and tugged her past Big Beaux. "Let's get *us* out of here."

"What? And leave Armond to die?"

"That's probably what he has in mind for us once he's done with us."

Josie followed him toward the front of the house, her weapon drawn. When they heard shouts, she stopped. "I can't abandon someone who's in danger, Connor. Not even a hardened criminal." She turned and headed toward the back of the house.

"Josie!"

She kept going. With a groan, Connor hurried after her. Did she have to go all noble right in the middle of an explosion? Of course she did. She struck him as solid on the honor system.

And because he was trying hard to learn that trait, and because she was cute and he'd enjoyed touching his forehead to hers earlier, he went after her. For all the above and to keep her alive, of course.

When they got to the back of the house, several guards were using fire extinguishers to put out the blaze from the explosion. Connor held Josie back as they took in the scene. Armond stood in the door of the huge master bedroom, a look of shock darkening his face. He wasn't responding to Big Beaux's coaxing him away.

"He usually goes to bed early," Beaux explained. "He's all shook up. Normally, he would have been in that bed by now."

"This is not good," Armond mumbled, disbelief evident in his scowl. "This is not good at all."

The enormous room had been destroyed. Beyond the fog of the fire extinguishers, the burgundy brocade curtains were now in charred shreds that whipped like dark tentacles reaching out in the wind. The massive bed had exploded like a bag of popcorn, white feathers and mattress stuffing covering the once-elegant comforter. The ceiling-to-floor windows were shattered and broken. And the whole room smelled dank and charred, the scent of burning wires merging with the smell of scorched furnishings and the chemical fumes from the fire extinguishers.

"What do you think?" Connor asked Josie.

She sniffed around like a hound dog, her pert nose up in the air. "I think someone called in a bomb."

"I got that," he said, glad she had a dry wit when needed.

"I also think Armond was right. Someone wants him dead."

She got in front of Armond's face. "We need to get you out of here. Now."

Beaux nodded. "I'm trying to persuade him."

She examined Armond with a quick frisking and a hand on his pulse. "You're confused and in shock, but you're alive. If you'd been in this bed asleep—"

Beaux gave her a fearful stare. "Sir, she's right. You're not safe here."

"Let's move, people," Connor called. Josie was taking notes on her phone. Or so she pretended. He figured she was calling this in to her boss. He poked her on the elbow and then called out, "Leave this the way you found it. The sooner we leave the better."

Josie gave him an overbearing frown but nodded.

Everyone went into action. Connor watched the lieutenants coming and going, but he also watched Josie. She studied each of the guards with such intensity her expression sizzled just like the drapes.

"What are you doing?" he whispered.

"Trying to find out which one of these men might want their boss dead," she replied. Then she turned to him. "Armond was right about this, and I think he might be right about something else."

"And what's that?"

"You could be next."

Connor shook his head. "I don't plan on that."

"You were his right-hand man for a long time, Connor. And he found out you were working for the FBI that whole time. That means someone thinks he could turn, too, since he was associated with you. Somebody is running scared, and they're taking names and going into action. First, his mistress, and now an attack on him. They know. They know the FBI has talked to him. His wife and son are in danger, too."

"I was careful," Connor retorted. "Very careful. But then, I've made a lot of enemies myself." He still wondered why Armond had let him live. Perhaps his reputation for being charming had impressed the old man.

"You know how that works. If they want you, they will find you," she said, her tone low and husky. "We need to get both of you out of here and into a safe house. Preferably by splitting you apart."

Connor paced while the worker bees took care of business.

"I don't get this. I witness the murder of his girlfriend, and he forces me to help and forces me to make this go away. And now he's running for his life. He could have killed me right there on the street, but he got in the car with me."

"Maybe he was in shock, as we saw when we

got here, or he took the first way out that came along. But whatever his motives, you're in this thing now. These people could already know that you and I are involved in covering this up. They'll come after us next."

Connor touched a hand to her arm. "You're in as much danger as I am."

"Possibly. Which is why we have to work together to find out who's behind this. And we start with his missing wife and that absent grown son."

"Do you think—"

"Just trying to cover all the bases."

She moved away and punched her phone.

This operation had gone from a cover-up to an official FBI investigation. Not just FBI. Make that the sheriff's department, an ATF team, the state police and the FBI. When something this big happened to a man like Louis Armond, everyone in law enforcement would want a piece of the action. And once again, Connor was in the thick of things. How could he possibly get out of this jam?

Maybe with Josie's help, if he could convince her to trust him.

He glanced from Louis Armond to the woman talking quietly on the phone. He had to protect Josie, whether she liked it or not. He'd brought her in on this, thinking they could both benefit from it.

Now he'd put her in danger.

The same way he'd put his sister in danger so many times.

He heard the sirens in the background and knew what he had to do. "Josie, we need to get out of here."

She nodded. "I've called in a report. We need to wait and give our statements to the locals and to our guys."

Connor glanced around. "And blow what little cover we have. If you're worried about one of Armond's minions being a snitch, then why do you want to stay around and talk to any law-enforcement officials? We can file our reports later."

He leaned close, nose to nose with her. "We're supposed to be here on a very secret, very important mission that doesn't involve the authorities."

She took one last long glance around the room. "Good point. So we have to take him with us and get him in a safe place. It's the only way to salvage this." Then she planted her ever-changing golden-green eyes on him. "It looks like you're the only person I *can* trust right now."

"Yes, sir. I understand, sir."

Josie turned from her phone and gave Connor a nod. Then she checked the hotel window for the third time. They were in an out-of-the-way boutique hotel close to the Garden District that had been cleared as one of their inner-city safe houses. Connor had a room across the hall from where Josie had an adjoining room with Armond. Big Beaux was watching over him, but Josie could see them through the open door. Connor had come over to join her.

"Sherwood is not happy with us," she said. She motioned him away from the adjoining door. "They found more than just an explosive device in that room. They also found a duffel bag full of cash—close to two hundred thousand dollars—and some invoices providing a month's worth of questionable shipments."

Connor's dark brows tipped up and he let out a low whistle. "Stolen and fake goods?"

She nodded. "They were shipped to a warehouse address on the river." Pointing to the address, she added, "Sherwood's got a team on the way there now. And he's coming after Armond. We don't need Armond's cooperation now. This is enough to bring him in."

Connor glanced back toward the other room. "This is a setup. Armond would never be that sloppy. He keeps his business records so hidden even I couldn't find them. And he never kept cash around the house. Where did they find this stuff?"

"Inside an open safe in the closet," Josie said. "Convenient, huh?"

"Too convenient."

Josie crossed the room to make sure Armond was where she'd left him. Connor followed. Whispering, she said, "So if things had gone right, Armond would have come home after the opera and gone to bed and then—boom. But why leave the evidence if you're trying to kill the man?"

Connor tugged at his curly hair. "Maybe the explosion was supposed to be a distraction while they emptied the safe? Or they purposely left the money and receipts for the FBI to find, whether Armond was alive or dead?"

"Or to implicate whoever happened to be here with him when the authorities came?"

"Which could have been me." Connor tapped his knuckles on the nearby desk. "This makes no sense. Maybe we should have hung around a little longer."

"That doesn't matter now. Sherwood plans to make it more sensible. He's on his way here, and he wants us gone once they take Armond."

"Gone? As in still undercover?"

"He needs us out there gathering information," Josie explained. "We have to stay here with Armond until we can swap him off to them. Sherwood wants us to do some more undercover work, ask around about Armond's contacts and enemies so we can build a case against him. Or find out who's after him."

Connor pushed at the tousled hair against his forehead. "And your superior is cool with us going into hiding together?"

It had been a long night for both of them, and Josie was too tired to lie to him. "Not that cool, but he agrees we can get more information if we stay undercover. And we can protect each other. So the plan is to keep my true identity from Armond while we dig for suspects."

"So we go to ground," Connor said. "It's not like I haven't done that before."

Josie saw the fatigue in his eyes. She'd never stopped to consider how much he had to look over his shoulder, either for the authorities or the criminals. But she refused to feel sorry for him and the double life he had been playing for the past couple of years. "Good. That means you'll follow my instructions and stay out of trouble."

"We're in a lot of trouble already," he said, staring out the hotel window. "What happens to Armond now?"

"After the FBI moves in and explains he's going into protective custody or possibly jail unless he'll cooperate?"

"Yeah, after that."

"He'll either turn and agree to testify against some of his enemies or his mysterious partner or . . . he'll be charged with transporting illegal and stolen goods into the country. He knows the risks, but he was willing to talk to us before this

70

happened." She checked the door again. "He'll be a little aggravated with us, too."

"Tough choices," Connor said. "But then the boys down at headquarters like to give out such ultimatums."

She propped on a nearby desk. "Is that how you came to be a part of our happy family?"

"More or less. I didn't have a lot of options."

"You can tell me about it all later," she said as she got up and stretched. "Let's go talk to Armond and tell him we have to leave him here so we can do some footwork."

"He won't be happy."

Josie texted a message to Sherwood and then waited while another undercover agent checked the hallway. Sherwood had placed his people all over the hotel.

"We can't guarantee his happiness, but if he wants our help, he'll agree. The man is running scared, and now we've found some evidence that could incriminate him."

"And of course, after we leave, the FBI will bully him into this deal based on that evidence. Makes you wonder who planted it."

She whirled from the door to answer another text, then went to the adjoining room. "Beaux, we're going to bring in another guard to make sure both of you are safe." When Armond lifted his head, about to protest, she said, "Don't even think about running, Mr. Armond. Two incidents in one night are enough to be sure someone is gunning for you. The guard will keep watch, and you need to stay right here for the next few hours."

Beaux nodded and patted his gun. "I won't let anybody near him." Then he sent a frowning glance toward his boss. "And I won't let him leave."

Armond's scowl grew wider. "Beaux, I'm still in charge."

"Not right now," Josie retorted. "That is, if you want to stay alive."

Josie walked back through the doorway between them and Armond and made sure she was out of earshot. Leaning in, she looked up at Connor. "They're in the building. It's time for us to sneak out." Then she frowned at Connor. "Hey, Randall, by the way, you seem to be wavering between loyalty to Armond and your duty to the FBI. So whose side are you really on?"

"Mine," he said with a shrug. Then he grabbed his wrinkled tux jacket and followed her out of the room. When she saw their relief guard coming toward them, Josie waited until the man went into the room she'd just left.

"We're clear," she told Connor. "Let's get out of here."

They'd made it to the back elevator down the hall and around the corner. Josie signaled to the guard waiting there to go down the hallway toward Armond's room. A couple of minutes later, the elevator doors opened and Josie stepped in, Connor right behind her. Then they heard shouting followed by gunshots.

"That sounded close to Armond's room." Josie drew her weapon. "Stay with me," she said on a hiss to Connor. She motioned him back around the corner.

"Where would I go?" he asked, his voice near her right ear. When he put his hand on her arm in a protective stance, she shook her head. "I'm going to get us out of this."

"And I'm going to make sure you stay alive."

In spite of the unnecessary gesture, she felt a little rip in her doubt of the man. He did have a way of being old-fashioned and debonair, even in a crisis. But right now, she needed him to stay behind her and follow her directions.

When more gunshots rang out, Connor stepped forward. "This isn't good. They've found Armond, Josie. We need to get out of here."

So he *was* only worried about his own sorry hide.

"I have to go back," she said, pushing him away. "My boss could be in that room."

"With Armond and whoever's shooting at him," Connor said, dragging her away from the area where the gunfire continued. "Josie, I'm serious. Sherwood is probably already dead. They'll ambush you."

Josie felt a solid need to defend her boss and the other agents who'd been working with them. She didn't have time to explain this to Connor. "I can't let my coworkers get mowed down."

The shots ended, and Connor tugged her into another open meeting room. "Shh. We'll figure something out."

"Let me go," she said, her mind on getting to her people. She'd started this whole thing by agreeing to help him. She had to see it through to the end, no matter what. "I have to—"

When a door down the hall burst open, Connor put a finger to his mouth. "Wait."

He pushed her behind him and peeked out the sliver of an opening in the door. Then he quickly shut the door, turned off the light and glanced at the balcony across the room. "Three of them and they're dressed for combat. We have to get out of here. Now."

Josie's shock changed to an automatic survival mode. "The windows?"

"Let's see. And hurry."

She followed Connor without hesitation now. Whatever he'd seen had put him into action. He tugged her into a circular alcove window covered with heavy curtains. "Stay still while I try to open this window."

Josie did as he asked, but she put her mind to work so she wouldn't panic. They were in a secluded luxury hotel. The meeting rooms were

74

all on the second floor near the guests' rooms and they each had a balcony to the street below. This was the only other way out. They'd chosen this hotel for its discretion and this floor for easy access to the street and parking garage.

With guards at each elevator and every door, how had anyone gotten in here?

Connor tugged at the heavy glass doors. "Not sure they're made to open. We don't have much time."

Josie heard the door from the hallway open. "We have to go now, Connor."

Connor grunted and let out a breath. "It's not budging."

Too late. She pulled him behind the curtain and held him close. "Don't breathe."

Connor covered her, his arms stretching to make both of them as tight and still as possible within the foot or so of the circular space. The air grew hot with tension. A cold sweat crawled like a clinging spider down her spine. Josie could hear footsteps, someone moving through the room. She watched through the haze of the heavy floral drapery and saw the silhouette of the lone gunman moving toward the curtain. She held her gun ready, her silent breath matching Connor's. One foot, another foot. She needed to breathe, to find some cool air. One more move and the gunman would be right on them.

And she couldn't hold her breath much longer.

The man stopped and stared. When his phone went off, Josie felt Connor shift close, saw the warning in his eyes. She wanted to gulp fresh air, but she couldn't. She had to stay still and crushed against Connor. He had her against the small alcove seat and he covered her like a shield. *Unnecessary, but comforting,* she thought in a wild, runaway logic that blocked her apprehension.

The lone man standing two feet away said something into the phone. Then he turned and stomped out of the room.

Josie sank into Connor. He pulled her tight against him and held her there, both of them taking deep breaths. "Are you all right?" he asked, his hand on her hair.

"No, I'm not all right," she said on a sharp inhale. "I'm sweating and I'm tired and I left a perfectly good pizza on the seat of my car last night."

Connor chuckled and let her go. "Could we run by your car and get it on the way out of here?"

Josie tugged the curtain open and pushed at her damp hair and then tried to put the feel of being in his arms out of her mind. "I'd like nothing better, but my car might be their next target."

He followed her into the shadows of the room and then turned back to the big sliding window. "We'd better try to get out this way. I don't trust the stairs or the elevators right now."

"What did that man say?" she asked. "It sounded like Italian."

Connor's expression went dark. "He told someone they'd taken care of the situation. Then something about a garage—the parking garage maybe."

"I guess that means they slaughtered everyone in that room. And they're still looking for something or someone."

"Josie, we can't go back into the hallway. They might still be lurking around to make sure they got everyone. Or they could be looking for us right now. Maybe they think we ran to the parking garage." He watched her and then said, "Let's get out of here, and we can circle back around to check, okay?"

Josie agreed with a nod. He was right. She just prayed she'd get a call from Sherwood. She followed Connor back to the big window and together they managed to pry the lock, both of them heaving and tugging until it slid open and they crashed against each other again.

A hot, humid night wind hit them, followed by the sounds of revelry down in the Square and traffic somewhere on Canal. Josie inhaled the smell of fried shrimp and freshly baked bread coming from a nearby restaurant.

Together, they climbed over the balcony and made the short drop to the ground. Connor dusted himself off, then took Josie's hand. "Let's get out of here."

They ran back toward downtown. "Let's get to the Square," Connor urged. "More of a crowd to hide in until we can get out of town."

But when they heard shouts, Connor tugged her back into a shadowed alley. "I don't think it's safe to go back."

Josie started forward, but a gunshot stopped her.

"Let's go," he urged. "We can do more good finding out who's behind this."

Josie reluctantly nodded her head. "Then let's get somewhere safe and start working this case."

An hour later they moved through the tourists crowding into Jackson Square. The sound of a lively jazz number spilled out of an open doorway down the street, followed by the smell of something spicy and tempting. Josie's stomach growled.

"I'm so hungry," she said, wishing she hadn't answered that phone last night. But this was her job, her life.

"Let's go," he said, his hand grasping hers. "I know a place out on the bayou where they have the best food in the world—pizza and po'boys and everything in between."

"Is it safe?" she asked, glad to follow him out of the stifling crowds. They'd backtracked up to Canal, and now he was weaving her in and out of the Quarter to throw off any followers.

"It will be if you're with me," he replied in that confident way that had her all mushy inside. Unnecessary, but this time she didn't argue with him.

SEVEN . . .

Josie's cell chimed as they later merged with the crowd on Decatur Street. When she saw the caller ID, she immediately answered. "Josie Gilbert."

"It's me, Gilbert."

"Agent Sherwood? You're alive?" She gave Connor a quick thumbs-up.

"Barely," her superior said with a groan. "Took a through and through in the left shoulder. They hit Armond with three bullets. He's in a coma. I'm with him at the hospital now. Undisclosed. We don't want the press blabbing his whereabouts. Got guards on him, too, but that big guard, Beaux, is on the run."

"And our other agents, sir?"

"One dead and one in critical condition."

Josie closed her eyes. "I should have been there."

"You did the right thing by getting Randall out of there. Stay with him. He's had eyes on

Armond for a while, so he might be our last hope to figure this out." He paused and then added, "Randall could be holding out on us. Try to get him to open up."

Josie didn't let on. "We'll stay undercover and out of sight until we hear differently," she said. "And, sir, I'll work on that suggestion."

"Good idea. And guard yourselves. These people mean business."

"I'll do my best. They came after Armond at his home and then found him in what we considered a safe location at the hotel. Could this be an inside job?"

"Who knows at this point, but yes, that's possible. We didn't get to question him or even arrest him. He'll hear the good news on that if he ever wakes up. Just keep reporting in so I won't have to worry about you, too."

"Yes, sir. We got out a window and circled back to the Quarter in a cab so we'd throw off anyone following us. Randall knows of a safe house out from the city."

"What about our other in-town designated safe house?"

"We think it might have been compromised, considering."

After a long pause, Sherwood said, "Do what you need to do to stay alive. I'll check back soon. Oh, by the way, before he passed out, Armond said something about a garage."

"Really? So did one of the hit men. We heard him, but he was speaking in Italian, so we can't be sure."

"Keep that in mind and check out any leads."

Josie hung up and gave Connor a nod. "Sherwood is okay. Got hit in the shoulder but it went through." She filled him in on Armond. "He's at the hospital with Armond, undisclosed location."

"We have a lot of medical centers and hospitals," Connor replied. "Why didn't he give you Armond's location? We still need to talk to him, find out what he wanted to tell me."

"Sherwood's trying to protect us, too," she explained. "He told me to stay with you. Oh, and he mentioned the garage—said Armond mumbled something about it before he passed out." She jotted some notes on her phone's notepad. "Maybe we should do a search of the parking garage back at the hotel."

"Or maybe another type of garage, like the big one back at the estate. But there are out-buildings all over that place. I know of one other one that has a classic car stored in it. We can't be sure which one everyone's talking about."

"You're right. I'll let the forensic and crime-scene techs handle that until Armond is conscious. Hopefully, he'll come clean."

"Unless we can figure something else out." He tugged her through the crowds crossing

Decatur between the Square and the Moonwalk. The Quarter was alive with music and laughter. The St. Louis Cathedral looked like a beacon in the wee hours of the night. "We threw them off but need to get out of town."

Josie agreed. Every face seemed sinister and ominous. She glanced over her shoulder with each turn, expecting a gunman to be following them. She noticed Connor doing the same. He was a distraction. And a partner now, since they'd been forced to team up. They were in this together, for better or worse.

Being an agent meant she always watched her back and stayed alert, but tonight she doubled that practice, her mind going back to the last time she'd been undercover. She'd missed one glaring sign that could have saved a young girl's life. Her informant's life. She wouldn't do that now, even if she thought saving Connor shouldn't be her concern. He was a human being, and he had been helpful in getting them out of that hotel and back to the Square. Sending out a prayer that the Lord would replace her judgmental attitude with one of wisdom, she followed Connor through the busy, crowded streets.

"Are they here?" she asked, her own instincts too blurred to pick up on anything out of the ordinary.

"I don't know," he said, his gaze roving over the streets. "I don't think they'd come into a crowd, but these people certainly are ruthless. Could be anyone, dressed like a tourist or a vendor. Let's head up Ursulines and take North Rampart back to Canal. Grab a cab and hope we've thrown them off."

"Not your fancy car?" Josie asked to take her mind off this horrible night.

"No. Too well-known around here."

"Aren't you too well-known around here, too?"

"Yeah. Which is why I'm going where no man in his right mind would venture."

"These men might not be in their right minds," she reminded him.

"Then we'll be waiting for them."

Connor had been running all of his life. He was used to running from the law, and lately, he'd learned to run from the bad guys, too. But having a too-bold, too-beautiful woman with him, now, that was different. Not that Josie was deadweight. She knew her stuff and watched and checked diligently as they moved through the shadows.

A beautiful, capable, tough woman who obviously had a strong code of ethics. And maybe a strong faith.

His sister had tutored Connor in that department, but he often wondered if God had heard Deidre's pleas on his behalf. Or his pathetic attempts to talk to God.

Now he thanked God for keeping them alive

and pulled out cash to pay the cab driver a hefty fare. They'd made it out of town but the route had been twisted and tiresome.

He glanced over at Josie, then tapped the taxi seat. "Stop here."

The cabby gave him a strange glance. "You sure? I mean, this ain't the best place to be on a Saturday night—er, make that an early Sunday morning."

"It's the best place for us," Connor retorted with a hundred-dollar bill. "And you never saw us."

"Man, I don't even tell people about this place," the cabby replied. "So I was never here."

Connor helped Josie out and straightened. "Dawn's coming." He pointed to the pink-tipped sun shining through the mossy cypress trees.

"Yes, I see," she replied. "And I'm so glad. Gives me a chance to really take in my surroundings." She did a complete turn. "This is sure some kind of resort, Randall. Have we reached the end of the earth?"

"Close," he said, eyeing the thick swampland and a couple of lean-to shacks on stilts. Early-morning humidity hung like brown gravy over the air. "This is a little-known tributary bayou off the Mississippi. Only outlaws and people who've reached the end of their rope come here."

"And you've been both?"

"And more," he replied. Then he took her hand. "But they know things that normal people haven't heard yet, so we might pick up some chatter regarding the Armond shooting. Besides, this place has the best French toast on earth."

Josie halted and shook her head and then pointed to the shack with the flashing neon sign. "You eat food in there?"

Connor slanted a glance at the run-down old building. The planked restaurant sat fat and swollen atop skinny stilts out over the water. The Crooked Nail lived up to its name. Every nail left in the place was either crooked or rusted out. Connor figured the grease from the fryer and the butter fumes from the griddle were the only things holding the place together. That and a mixture of humanity that rivaled the full-flavored gumbo.

"Yes, I've had a lot of meals here. Mama Joe knows how to make a mean bouillabaisse."

Josie looked skeptical. "I'm okay with coffee, but I don't want to drink any swamp mud."

"The coffee is black and strong, but Mama Joe makes it with fresh water. And maybe a little swamp mud."

He led her up the crusty shell-covered path to the wide, planked front porch that served as part of the restaurant and bar. "We can kick back here and regroup." He motioned toward another building nearby. "Mama Joe's Bed and Breakfast, bayou-style."

Josie gasped at the sight of the other squatty

house that seemed to be low and floating until she realized it was a boathouse, then gave him a hard stare when they hit the last step. "That's not exactly a hotel. It's a boathouse. You're always luring me out into the boonies, Connor. Why is that?"

He leaned close and winked. "Maybe I want you all to myself."

Her eye roll didn't offer much hope. Swatting at mosquitoes, she said, "Just get me the coffee, Randall."

Josie woke with a start. She'd heard a splash. Blinking, she glanced around the tiny room Mama Joe had put her in early this morning after feeding them a huge platter of that famous French toast. According to the height of the sun, it must be noon. She'd slept about six hours.

The bed was comfortable and clean, and the gentle rocking of the old boathouse had lulled her into a deep sleep. She was forever thankful for that. The heavy screens on the two windows allowed for a nice warm breeze, and the squeaky old ceiling fan had hung on for another night to keep her from sweating to death. The boathouse was all cypress planks and creaking floors with a primitive decor that spoke of eccentricity and a bit of artistic flair. Bright colors in the furniture and the bedspread and curtains took away from the gloom of the weathered wood. And since the sheets smelled like sunshine, Josie decided she could probably stay here forever just rocking with the tide.

But her mind wouldn't let her do that. She got up and rinsed off in the tiny bathroom somewhat attached to the bedroom. The swag suite, as Connor had called it, at least had running water.

When she came out of the bathroom, she heard masculine laughter out on the old dock between the boathouse and the restaurant. Josie went to one of the wide windows and squinted through the hot-pink blossoms of a bougainvillea vine.

Connor. Fishing? Could he really be that relaxed after last night? She took her time studying him, interested in spite of her better judgment.

He looked young and carefree, his hair tousled and windblown, his beard just over a five-o'clock shadow. He wore a blue chambray shirt and old worn jeans. And he was barefoot.

Adorable. And so different from the man she'd studied and condemned as shallow and unsavory. He didn't look unsavory or shallow right now. He looked good. Too good for a woman who hadn't had any caffeine.

No. Not adorable. Not attractive. Not intriguing.

She needed to get her head together. So she threw on the lavender-scented clothes that had mysteriously appeared on the high-backed chair by the door and went looking for food and drink.

The flared jersey skirt was old but clean, and

the softly faded T-shirt had a butterfly printed on the front. Someone with flower-child tendencies must have owned these clothes once. Since she had no idea where her other clothes had landed, Josie was glad her gun was still lying on the old dresser by the bed.

She went to put it on and realized her shoulder holster had gone missing. Leaving the gun on the dresser, she hurried out to the restaurant. The smell of bacon frying and coffee perking made her mouth water.

But the way Connor turned and smiled at her through the veil of Spanish moss hanging from the old cypress trees made her insides turn as mushy as the dirt bank down near the swamp water. Telling herself she had a case to work, Josie gave herself a strict and silent talking-to.

"How ya doing this fine morning?" Mama Joe asked after Josie entered through the back screen door. The restaurant was more of an old family home with a big kitchen and dining area. Mama Joe apparently lived in the back rooms.

"I'm . . . uh . . . good, all things considered," Josie replied. Last night this place had seemed like a dump. But in the bright light of midday, it wasn't half-bad. Quaint and colorful in a folksy way, the restaurant looked a lot like the tiny four-room boathouse. Old road signs and license plates lined the planked walls right along with colorful paintings and signs printed with sage bits of advice. Some people had even left hand-printed messages on the walls.

A crudely scrawled verse from Proverbs, Chapter Four, caught Josie's attention:

Keep thy heart with all diligence: for out of it are the issues of life.

Mama Joe watched as Josie silently read the sign. "Are you a heart girl?"

"Excuse me?" Josie asked as she took the mug of coffee the older woman offered.

"Your eyes, they speak of the heart," Mama Joe said, bangles and beads rattling against her wrist. She grinned and twirled a strand of bright gold hair that matched her one gold tooth. "But your head, it tells you to guard your heart, *oui*?"

"Maybe," Josie retorted. "I guess I'm more of a head girl. I use my brain to guard my heart." She couldn't stop herself from glancing out the window toward the dock.

"You might consider letting go that notion," Mama Joe said in her singsong part Creole, part Caribbean accent. She dressed with the same vivid colors as her decor, all scarves and fabric, like a patchwork personality.

Josie stared out the window at Connor. "I can't do that." She got up and grabbed a golden biscuit stuffed with ham off the stove. The crusty bread tasted buttery and the ham was tender-sweet. "Put this on his tab, please."

Mama Joe chuckled and shuffled back behind the counter.

Josie bit into the fat biscuit and chewed the buttery dough before stopping in midstep to take a long sip of the coffee.

"Hey, sleepyhead," Connor called, motioning for her to join him on the dock. "Save me a bite of that, will you?"

"I'm eating all of it," Josie replied. She glanced at the chipped mug in her hand. A grinning red crawfish wearing a straw hat greeted her and made her smile. She really shouldn't feel in such a carefree, vacation kind of mood.

"We have things to do," she said to Connor to counter that feeling.

"I know." His expression turned serious. "Mama Joe has put out some feelers." He laid down his pole and helped her across the creaky, unreliable dock. "But for now, we rest."

"I have to figure this out," she said, her brain already annoying her with questions.

"I've been thinking about things all night," he said. Then he nipped a piece of the biscuit right out of her hand. "I have some of the names we need to research." He pointed to a small pocket-size notepad. "Since Armond never finished his own list."

"Names? Of people who might have it in for Armond and you?"

"Yes." He sat down on an old wooden bench

and nibbled his bit of biscuit. "He was too scared, too sure someone was coming for him, as if he'd been expecting this. This has to be the work of a rival boss or someone who has more power than Armond. Maybe even the partner he refuses to name. Which I didn't think was possible. But if this person heard a rumor that Armond was turning, well . . ."

"I agree." She drank some more coffee and took her time looking out over the black bayou waters. A shiver moved down her spine in spite of the warm day. Alligators and snakes and all kinds of creatures lived in that brackish water. It made her think of crime scenes and dead, lifeless bodies. Bad memories. A haze of intuition pushed at her upbeat mood. "My phone has no bars out here."

"That can work in your favor right now."

"No traces, no GPS?"

"Exactly. This spot is way off the grid."

"And how did you find it?"

He shooed a fly out of the way. "I've been undercover in some strange places," he explained. "A drug deal brought me here. Back when I was on the other side of the law."

A drug deal had done her in at the Dallas division. "You used to deal drugs?"

"No. I just got caught up with some people who did. But they are all behind bars now."

"And how did you get away so easily?"

"I never said it was easy. They beat me up and

left me for dead. I washed up on this shore half-dead and freezing. Mama Joe took me in and nursed me back to humanity."

Not back to health but back to humanity. Interesting. Maybe this was the place where he'd had an epiphany, a change of heart. "That bad, huh?"

"It's not the first time I've been left for dead."

"How do you live like that?"

"I don't. Not anymore. This place was the beginning of my restoration. I'm trying to get past my past."

"Aren't we all?" She finished her food and drained the coffee, recording his admission for a later conversation. "We need to get to work, Connor."

"I want to hear about *your* past," he replied, his direct stare unnerving her.

She pulled herself back together. "You know about my past. You're too good at what you do."

"I know what's on paper. But I want to know what's in your head."

She grinned, pointed a finger at him. "Not right now. Not when we need to figure out who's after Armond."

"And us."

"And us," she repeated. "I really don't like that part."

"Me, either."

He lifted her up with his left hand on her arm.

"Let's go inside. You never know what might wash up out of these dark waters."

Josie glanced around at the tall cypress trees knotted together in clumps around and in the water and the thick palmetto palms nestled underneath scrawny pines and scrub oaks. The air dripped with a hot, humid wind. The trees shifted and stretched with a lazy lift here and there, the clinging gray moss serving as a curtain. The palms swayed in a secretive dance. She caught a whiff of jasmine and honeysuckle, mixed with decay and wet earth.

Was someone out there, waiting to kill them?

She turned back to Connor and wondered if she'd trusted the wrong man after all.

EIGHT . . .

"So we're pretty sure Armond has this silent partner for some of his dealings, and Mama Joe's boys have confirmed that they've heard that rumor for years," Connor explained later between bites of a shrimp po'boy sandwich. "He never gave me a name, but I always wondered what the deal was there. And me being me, I wanted to crack that mystery, but I searched that house and used every tactic I knew but I've never found anything—no phone records, no computer files, not even a flash drive."

Josie nibbled on her own chicken-salad sandwich and gave him a skeptical glance. "Are you sure? What if Armond wanted you to believe that he had someone else ordering him around? I'm sure he has shell corporations all over the world."

They were alone on the back porch of the restaurant with churning brown water below them and a rusty, wobbling ceiling fan over their heads. Connor had been on watch most of the day, just waiting for some stranger to walk into the Crooked Nail and mow them down. But Mama Joe had posted her own brand of protection all through the swamp. Big men with big dogs and shotguns and powerful rifles they used to kill alligators and wild hogs.

Josie had been on alert, too. She did the visual thing several times over. She still didn't trust him, Connor realized. It was midafternoon and she'd heard nothing from Sherwood. Of course, they didn't have the best phone service out here. They'd have to leave soon enough, but this was the safest resting place he could find.

He answered her question. "He does have hidden assets, bank accounts in Switzerland and the Cayman Islands, but this is different. This person, whoever he or she is, is so hidden it's like looking for gold on the side of a mountain. Hard to see."

"And he wants it that way," Josie countered, her cat eyes giving him that slant of disbelief. "We need to remember Louis Armond is a criminal."

"I keep that in mind every day," Connor retorted. "And I need to remember you're FBI."

"I'll remind you of that every day," she countered.

"You're antsy," he noted, giving her the once-over. She looked cute in the flowing skirt and T-shirt but she also looked different. Not so uptight and buttoned-up. Even her precise, long-ish bob had gone all curly from the humidity. She didn't seem so on the job and *let's get the bad guys* right now. The gun in her room proved that more than enough without her showing it.

"Mama Joe says word of Armond's dead mistress is all the buzz in New Orleans. Everyone's wondering if a hostile takeover is about to ensue. But no one's talking about why or who or what. So we've got nothing. Except that we're on someone's radar. One of my informants told me this was bigger than Armond and the FBI put together, but he refused to say who, what, when and where. A lot of talk and most of it not so good."

"I just love keeping company with you," she said on a tease. "But we've got work to do."

"So what's the plan?" he asked her, figuring she already had a plan.

"The way I see it, we have to find out who's

trying to kill Louis Armond so we can save us, too. We also need to find out who this silent partner is, and if he or she is real, once and for all. It only makes sense that the partner has heard about Armond's possible turn and of course they are not happy," she said, all business now. Even if she was barefoot.

"Agreed," he said.

"Now tell me about anyone else you might suspect."

"His wife," Connor said. "Vanessa Armond likes the lifestyle Louis provides, so she's turned her head too many times after seeing him photographed with models and showgirls."

"Such as Lewanna?"

"Yes, the now-very-dead Lewanna."

"You think his own wife ordered a hit on the girlfriend and then him? But why, if she's used to his philandering nature?"

"A woman scorned," he said on a shrug. "Maybe she's just had enough. It happens. And she'd stand to inherit millions." He leaned forward, his elbows on the table. "Especially if she has decided to run off with the silent partner, or at least make a play for the other man. Or she could actually be the silent partner, the one who really calls the shots. She'd stand to inherit if Armond is dead. And . . . she'd also want me dead because she thinks I know too much."

A splash in the water made both of them glance

up. "If she's found out you're FBI, she'd want you dead, too."

Josie's eyes turned a rich gold-green. "Yes, it certainly does make sense when you put it that way. Money talks. Dirty money really talks. People will kill for that reason alone."

"Are you thinking of your mother?" he asked, sincere now for once and wanting to get inside her psyche a little bit.

"Are you asking me about my mother?" she replied with a deflection maneuver he recognized.

"Yes."

Josie stared out over the rich stream of dark water. "She loved a man who turned out to be a criminal. She turned the other cheek to stay with him, no matter what. Now she's broke and bitter and living in a one-bedroom condo in Atlanta." She shrugged. "Honestly, I'm surprised she didn't do something desperate long ago to make him stop, but she's still alive even if she is heart-broken." She shivered and did her eagle-eyed visual again. "I don't want to ever be like that."

Ah, now they were getting to the heart of the matter.

"And you resent her and all such criminals as your father, right?"

She turned and gave him a direct glance. "Yes."

"So you resent me and all I stand for."

"Yes."

So much for that together time when they'd

bonded last night. He'd held her close, sniffed her lemony perfume and wondered what it'd be like to kiss her. Killer, from her point of view and the disapproving slant of her eyes.

"I can't convince you I've changed," he said. "So I'll just try to show you."

"You have convinced me, a little bit," she replied, surprising him. "You could have left me here last night and gone away. But you stayed."

The thought had crossed his mind, but he'd shooed it away with the mosquitoes. He couldn't leave this woman behind. He made light of it now. "For the French toast, yes."

She actually laughed at that. And made his heart do a whirl that ran deeper than the water's current. Seeing her face light up and her eyes dance could make him stay a lot longer than any French toast. But it would be just as sweet.

"Did you think I'd abandon you?" he asked, his eyes holding hers. "That I'd just run away to save myself?"

"When we first got here, yes. But I didn't really think about anything after my head hit the pillow. And I didn't think about it when I woke up and heard you laughing. If you'd left, I would have found you."

"I believe that," he said, glad for her bluntness.

"Now that we've settled that, why don't we go over everything you know about this silent partner?"

"I know nothing." He finished his sandwich, inhaling the crispy French bread with a satisfied sigh. "Armond really doesn't trust anyone, so I had to draw him out. I think I'm only alive today because I helped him find the Benoits. He had to put up a fight regarding my fun time with the FBI to make himself look good, but surprisingly no one came forward and did me in. Now this."

He threw a chunk of bread to a couple of wood ducks roaming the shore. "I didn't give him up to the FBI because we really didn't have anything to pin on him. He's meticulous about hiding incriminating paperwork, but I've got a few hunches to play out. On the other hand, all the intel I was able to get is sitting on someone's desk back at your office. The FBI left me twisting in the wind with a possible hit on my head."

"The paintings are worth millions," she said. "Could this be about the Benoits, then?"

"I don't think so. He's got them out on tour in a few select museums that are highly guarded and airtight. If anyone wanted the paintings, they'd hit the museums and art galleries first."

She gave him a sideways glance, her hair falling like dark feathers over her cheek. "Art crime ranks high on the FBI list. I'm guessing you daydreamed about how to break that airtight security, right?"

He couldn't deny it. "The Benoits are tempting, but if I wanted to steal his art, I could take my pick of the pieces in his mansion. Old habits die hard, but I'm done with taking what doesn't belong to me." He looked her in the eye. "Anything I acquire from here on out will be mine, legally and completely."

She lifted a dark brow at that comment and probably at the way he was looking at her now. He'd daydreamed about her a lot, too, over the past few hours. But Josie Gilbert wasn't someone who could be acquired. She was strong and sarcastic and a bit cynical. But lovely in a tough-girl way.

And not good for him to be around.

He longed for his old FBI partner. Not one bit of temptation there, if you didn't count the doughnuts and chocolate cake that the big man had always shared. But his former "keeper" had retired at the required age of fifty-seven and was now fishing somewhere in Florida.

Connor could go for that kind of life right now.

Then he changed that and longed for someone like the woman who'd trusted him to stay. The woman who'd vowed to find him if he had left. The woman sitting here with him now, her mind razor-sharp and snapping, her ambition as strong and urgent as his own. New territory.

This was one of those ironic moments in life. He had a huge crush on a woman who could cart him off to jail with one wrong move, and they were running from people who could kill both of them, all because he'd blown his cover with a crime boss, then convinced that boss to let him hang around. Where was the justice in that? Justice, maybe. A challenge? Definitely.

"What about Armond's son?"

She'd managed to get his head back in the game, just like that.

"Lou lives in Europe. A good life filled with yachts, mansions and red-carpet moments with actresses and models."

"Like father, like son."

"Yes, Lou supposedly runs Armond's philanthropic organizations."

"He has philanthropic tendencies?"

"He has money to hide or get rid of for tax purposes, yes. He made a big contribution to Princess Lara's house-building project in New Orleans. For what it's worth, Armond told me repeatedly that he'd made enough money to come clean and live legitimately."

"So why didn't he?"

"His smuggling operation is too easy to give up. And too secret for me to crack into. I'm telling you those receipts and that money—that was put there by someone who wanted to implicate him."

"One of his own?"

"I don't know. He pays his people well for discretion and for security. None of them are hurting and Lou is set for life."

"Hmm. Somebody wants a piece of the pie."

"Or the whole enchilada."

"Do you think Lou would off his own father?"

"Money is motive, sweetheart," he said, knowing it to be true. His workaholic mother had lived for money and had died at gunpoint on a dark street, leaving Deidre and him with mounting charge-card bills and no money to pay for any of her debts.

Josie must have picked up on his dark tone. "I'm sorry about your mother. Bad way to die."

"Mugged and shot," he said, the memories of that night hitting him with the humidity. "Deidre never quite got over her death."

"And you? You became a criminal to provide for your sister?"

"At first. I wanted to be noble like Robin Hood, but the power overtook me. Like mother, like son. She pretended to have it all together, and I've pretended to be someone I'm not."

"But you're making up for it now, right?"

"I'm trying. Enforced nobility is the closest thing to being noble. So here I am living on the honor system, when really, I have no honor."

"You're a work in progress, Connor."

"Maybe so."

They'd stared at each other while they crossed another boundary. Did she finally get that he was trying? He prayed so.

"Let's jot down names and arrange facts," she

said, taking the drawing paper Mama Joe had given her and placing it on the gray, weathered picnic table. "Maybe we can piece together some means and motive."

"You know how to get to a guy's heart, Agent Gilbert," he replied with a hand over his chest.

"I'm a work in progress, too," she said.

Four hours later, Mama Joe put a huge piece of fried chicken on Connor's dinner plate, and they still hadn't narrowed down one good suspect, just pieces of key people around Armond.

"Now, eat up," Mama Joe said with false huffiness. "If you gotta run, you sure gonna need some fuel to get you going."

"This is our third meal today," Josie noted. "I haven't eaten this much in years."

Connor dipped mashed potatoes and lathered them with rich brown gravy. "Good thing I only swing by once or twice a year."

"Your girl there needs some meat on her bones," Mama Joe said as if Josie wasn't at the table. "Feed that girl, Connor. I know you know all about what goes with what and all that fancy cooking, but this girl needs some nourishment for the soul."

"I'll take another corn-bread muffin, then," Josie said, pointing toward the always-on stove at the back of the restaurant. "And some more of that crawfish-and-corn chowder."

"It's bisque," Connor corrected with a grin. "But I'll have some, too."

Mama Joe put her hands on her ample hips. "Y'all see the stove. Help yourself. Me, I got to get off these tired feet and watch *NCIS* reruns."

"She's got a thing for Mark Harmon," Connor pointed out.

"Don't we all?" Josie jumped up and served herself in a true native way that made him laugh.

They'd be leaving at dark, starting with a pirogue ride through the swamp and moving on to a pickup truck hidden in some bramble somewhere on the other side of the bayou. This place had a system of getting people in and out and gone before any lawmen or angry men could find them. And Connor had already lingered too long. The shadows stretching toward the water could hold people who were willing to shoot all of them.

"So we have a plan," Josie replied when she came back to the table. "We have to start at the beginning, which means the main estate and the garage. You think we might find something on the silent partner there?"

"Yes. He closeted himself in the office there a lot. We start back at the mansion on the river, move to his penthouse in New Orleans if we need to, and we might have to take a quick jaunt to Europe."

"The bureau won't let you leave the country, Connor."

"But you might."

"Hey, we're not that comfortable with each other. I can't allow that, so don't even tease about it."

"I am teasing," he said, not teasing. He'd do whatever he had to do to get out from under the yoke of Armond's weighty pseudo-friendship. He had to think of Deidre, and now he had to think of Josie. She wouldn't like that, but it wasn't his nature to put women in harm's way. An old-fashioned notion but one he couldn't break. He should have been there with his mom the night she died, but he'd been out looking for a good time.

Too late to make up for that mistake.

Never too late to learn from that mistake.

And as Mama Joe would tell him, never too late to pray for forgiveness and start all over with a born-again attitude.

Could he start fresh? He planned to do just that once this case was solved.

But first, he had one more question to ask Josie.

"What happened in Dallas?"

She dropped her buttered corn-bread muffin and sat openmouthed. "What does that matter now?"

"You obviously had to get out of Texas. I need to understand why." He'd wondered about that all day. They might get into some heavy stuff before this was over. He wanted her to be prepared. He couldn't have her falling apart on him.

His common sense told him that wouldn't happen, but he needed to put up a wall between them so he wouldn't get distracted.

Right now she looked aggravated, her expression heating up with a mad shine. "Is that a deal breaker, Randall? Do you demand a clean working record with all your handlers?"

"It might be an issue. I can't have you choking on me."

She glared at him over her sweet tea. "Are you serious? I mean, I've pretty much forgiven you all of your shortcomings, not to mention sticking my neck out to help you with Armond. And I trusted you not to leave me out here in this isolated swamp, and now you decide to interrogate me?"

"I just want to know," he said. "Nothing to do with this Armond stuff. Just what happened."

She gave him a look that caused the butter on her muffin to slide right off. "I don't have to explain that to you."

"Defensive, aren't we?"

"Seriously, are you messing with my head for a reason?"

He leaned forward, twirled his straw in his tea. "Yes. You have my file, so you know my weak spots. C'mon, you answered when I asked about your mother, so I know you've overcome that. This has to be something else."

"And you have to know this right now?"

"You answered about your mother right away. But you didn't say much about your daddy. The one who's in prison."

Her skin paled. "Because you know about that. And you probably know about Dallas, too."

He wouldn't lie. "I was about to do some digging when Armond stepped back into my life. Now here we are."

"I don't want to talk about Dallas," she said, dropping her spoon. "Let's get on with our plans. I have to brief my supervisor."

So Dallas was a sore spot. He'd find out, one way or another. He'd be more discreet next time he brought up the subject. "Let's get going, then," he said.

He turned to gather their empty plates to take inside. He'd made it to the screen and held it open, waiting for Josie to cross the big porch, when the first shots came whizzing through the air. One of the shots hit a plate he held and shattered it.

And the next one hit the table where Josie had been sitting. But he didn't see her anywhere.

NINE . . .

Josie's side hitched as she slid onto the deck of the boathouse and plunged through the screened door. Her gun. She'd left it in the bedroom. Scooting on her knees, she grabbed her weapon and unlocked the safety, then checked the ammo. Then she slid to the window and stared out into the growing dusk.

Connor? She didn't know where he'd gone. When she'd heard the first shot, she'd gone into automatic mode and had ripped through a side door off the porch, bullets blasting all around her. Then she'd followed the cypress trees toward the boathouse, glad for the draping moss that served as a cover in the shadows.

Now she had to get back out there and protect Connor. When she heard several more shots echoing through the thicket of cypress trees, she did a visual of her surroundings, but in the dimming light, she couldn't tell which shapes were human and which were nature.

Josie inhaled a deep, calming breath, the sound of bullets hitting across the way forcing her to stay down.

Then everything went silent. The whole place

had gone eerily quiet. Even the trees didn't move.

A creaking groan hit the deck of the boathouse. Josie sucked in a breath and held herself still, her back against the rocking wall. Holding her gun out, she steadied her finger on the trigger, ready to shoot.

Footsteps dragged through the boathouse, slow and quiet. The swamp became deadly silent. Not a bird chirping, no splashes in the water. No music in the dance hall. No more shots deep in the woods. Silent, still, holding its breath.

In the same way she was holding hers.

Where was Connor?

Her heart pounded so loudly, she was sure someone out there was listening and following the beat. She was trapped in this stifling little room. All she could do was wait and hope that everyone was safe. That Connor was safe.

But she wouldn't go down without a fight. She held her gun steady and remembered her training.

The partially closed door creaked in protest as it swung open. Then a big dark man wearing overalls stood there with what looked like a souped-up shotgun.

Josie stared up at him, her gun trained on his forehead. "Stop or I'll drop you right where you stand."

The big man put a finger to his lips. "Shh. I'm Toby. Mama Joe sent me to find you."

Josie staggered up the wall, her gun still drawn. "How can I be sure?"

He held the shotgun down. " 'Cause if I don't fetch you back to the meetin' place, Mama Joe will put a load of buckshot in my backside."

She stood but didn't let her guard down. "Well, when you put it like that—"

"C'mon," he said, the shotgun still pointed down. "We got some unwanted visitors. But we got it under control for now."

"Where is Connor?" Josie asked, her eyes adjusting to the growing darkness. She could make out the trees and the water, but the whole swamp was shrouded in gray shadows that danced like skeleton bones around the boathouse.

"Follow me," Big Toby replied without giving her any answers.

He didn't take her gun away, so that was good. She'd shoot him if he turned on her. But the giant didn't turn on her or try to harm her in any way. Instead, he took her through a path that didn't begin to look like a path. He swatted palmetto fronds and cypress limbs and climbed over knotty cypress knees then helped her through.

"We're going the wrong way," she tried to point out. "The Crooked Nail is right by the boat-house."

"We on the right path, lady," he said through a grin.

The woods grew cooler in the gloaming, but the bugs grew bigger and bolder. Josie slapped at her skin and longed for air-conditioning and a good shower. She didn't even want to consider snakes and alligators. "Where are we going?"

"Shh." Toby held her behind him, then whistled.

Josie waited, glad for the cover but confused about what exactly they were doing in this soup bowl of humidity and humming, hungry creatures.

An answering sound echoed over the still woods.

"Let's go," Big Toby said, still protecting her with each step.

Finally, they reached a clearing, and she saw what must be the pirogue Connor had told her about earlier. "Where is he?"

"I'm right here," Connor said from the shadows. "Hurry."

Josie mowed around Toby and hurried to the boat, relief washing her in a hot glow. "Are you all right?"

Connor stood behind a giant cypress tree. A few yards away, two more men stood guard with Mama Joe. Even though she had her own big gun, too, Mama Joe stepped forward with a package. "Your clothes. I cleaned them."

Apparently, the swamp had its own code of justice and a washing machine, too. Josie didn't want to ever be on the bad side of these people.

But right now, she thanked God for them.

"I'm fine," Connor said as he pulled her close. "I was worried about you but then I figured you'd gone for your gun."

"Yes." She still had the safety off. Suddenly, she didn't trust anybody. "Yes. I'm okay."

He reached out and brushed damp hair off her forehead. "Don't ever scare me like that again, Agent Gilbert."

Josie swallowed, tried to breathe. The humidity was doing strange things to her. She felt hot and faint and disoriented.

Or maybe it was the way Connor was looking at her. His eyes held hers, roving, searching, sending her some sort of message.

"Let's go," she said, trying to find her business persona again. Trying to stop her heart from jumping out of her chest.

"We've got supplies and we're ready," he said. He guided her to the squat little boat and sat her on a narrow bench seat. "We have an escort waiting at the next pickup site."

"How will we get out of here?" she asked, glancing around. The water and woods were already drenched in darkness. The big live oaks and cypress trees loomed like gray giants standing in a cluster.

"By memory," he said. Then he took a long wooden pole and pushed it off into the murky black water, a tiny battery-powered light rigged at the front of the boat his only guide. Josie sank down on her seat and saw Big Toby standing on the shore, watching them. He waved to them. Josie waved back, then saw Mama Joe on the shore.

"We'll pray you home," Mama Joe called, her hand up in farewell.

That gave Josie some comfort while she sat there wondering how Connor would ever find his way out of this inky, wet blanket of darkness.

A few minutes later, Connor turned the boat down a narrow channel. He knew this route by heart, but it was still hard to see much past the bow of the boat. A light off in the distance beckoned. The next pickup point.

"We're almost there," he told Josie. She'd been quiet. Too quiet.

"Who were they?" she asked, her mind obviously putting things back together.

"Two armed men, dressed in camouflage. They got a little too close, but Mama Joe's guys tracked them. Got off several shots before they got away."

"They got away?"

"Yep. The boys had them cornered up by the road. But they managed to escape through a heavy thicket of trees. We heard an engine roaring, so they had a truck waiting."

She let out a frustrated breath. "So we don't

have any evidence and no way of identifying them."

"No. And no reliable eyewitnesses, since it was dark and they blended in with the swamp." He moved the long pole back and forth. "What we can assume is they weren't here for the social hour. They knew we were here and they came to kill us. And one of them is a bad shot or I'd be dead right now."

"I thought you were," she said, her words hollow and quiet.

"I worried about you, too," he said. He'd never admit how his heart had stopped and his chest had tightened at the thought of what these people would do to her if they caught her.

"We have to go back to Armond's mansion," she said, all business now. "We should have searched the place more when we were there. And we need to find out if he's out of the coma so we can question him."

"He could be talking already." Connor thought about that. "I wonder if Sherwood and all the different forensic teams found anything." He wondered, too, if they'd cooperate with each other. This was not the time for the different law-enforcement divisions to go territorial.

Josie's response was low but firm. "If we ever get back to civilization, I can find out."

"Armond could tell us, if he'll talk at all."

"Or he could be dead."

Connor managed to calm himself into thinking ahead. When he'd heard those shots and looked up to find her gone, his mind had swirled with deadly scenarios. He didn't like these protective feelings. She could take care of herself, and yet, he wanted to take care of her. He'd never felt like that with anyone except his sister. He'd never let things go too far with anyone, with any woman. New territory. New challenges.

"That was close," he finally said. "But now we don't have to wonder anymore. They want us, too. Preferably dead."

"Too close. I had to get to my gun."

"I know. Instincts."

"Yes. And survival mode."

"It's okay. We're here now."

He drifted the pirogue up onto the shoreline, his work as silent as the veiled trees. Those goons had escaped, but they could be lurking about. They'd found Josie and him somehow.

But how?

Who would know how to get to this isolated end of the earth?

Somebody who knew his movements and had anticipated that he'd come here first? Armond didn't know about the Crooked Nail. Very few people did.

Had someone put a bead on Josie, a tracker on her phone maybe? Or was someone besides the FBI following his every move? He'd believed even Sherwood and his team wouldn't find Josie and him out here. But somebody sure had.

He'd have to talk to Josie about that later. Right now, he needed to get them in that truck and out of this swamp. He secured the boat, then helped her over onto the bank. "Let me check the vehicle and our escort first."

She held her gun with both hands, her whole stance on high alert. "I'll be right here."

Connor crept up the bank and whistled. After an answering whistle, a lone gunman walked out of the woods across from the truck.

"All clear," the man called. "We'll lead you outta the swamp." Then he disappeared back into the shadows.

Connor went to the waiting truck and tugged at the palm fronds. Then he reached under the driver's-side front tire and found the key. "Josie, it's okay."

She emerged from the trees and went around to the passenger side. Soon they were both in the old truck.

"What now?" she asked, fatigue circling her words. She probably didn't like having to rely on him.

Connor waited until he saw taillights up ahead, then cranked the truck and turned toward a bumpy dirt lane.

"We find out if Armond's alive and talking. If he is, we go back to New Orleans and see if he'll talk to us. If he's not alive, we go to the mansion and dig through his files."

"Sherwood will want me back in New Orleans, either way," she whispered. "He'll want both of us back to file a report."

"So you'll obey him blindly?"

"I didn't say that," she retorted. "He might have information from the explosion. Or we might have to figure this out on our own."

Connor smiled into the darkness. Josie was her own woman, no matter who tried to control her. That could be a good thing, since he wondered if their problem stemmed from someone within the FBI.

Josie tapped End on the call she'd just had with Special Agent Sherwood and turned to Connor. "The only other bit of evidence they found at the mansion was the source of the bomb. Enough C-4 to blow up the bed, using the lightbulb in the lamp to do the job. Someone managed to get inside that fortress and set up that bomb and possibly plant the money and the shipment receipts. I'm thinking it had to be an inside job."

Connor turned toward the window. They were in a hotel room high above the city, waiting for word from Sherwood on how to proceed from here. From this view, Connor could see the Mississippi River below. A steamboat full of tourists plowed through the muddy water right next to a barge bulging with imports. A couple holding hands strolled along the Moonwalk.

As usual, he was trapped in a prison of his own making.

He glanced back at Josie. "Which means we have to go out there and look around. With new eyes."

"Connor, Sherwood was firm. They covered every inch of the mansion and brought in a laptop and several electronic pads. The few files they found on those were clean. What they found in the safe is it. Armond obviously has most of his dirty work hidden. And whoever tried to kill him, well, they didn't leave any tracks but they did leave that load of cash and that stack of invoices."

"So you don't think that was Armond's stash?"

"I can't be sure until I talk to Armond, but I'm guessing no. The whole explosion thing would have brought the authorities even if we hadn't been there. They got in, left the evidence and set up the bomb. No tracks, but plenty to stew about."

"There's always tracks," he replied. "And I'm the kind of person who knows every trick to hide those tracks. I used to hide mine. If I'd had more time, I would have eventually found Armond's hiding places."

"And that's why we keep you close now," she reminded him.

Connor turned back to the view. "I've always loved this city," he said. "The first time I came here as a kid, I knew I wanted to live here." He put his hands in his pockets. "My mother lived here before I was born and we only came back for a few months when I was around ten years old, but she never talked about it much." He kept his back to Josie. "She had a place here. Owned it free and clear. It's mine now."

Josie got up and came to stand by him. "Where's your apartment?"

He turned to look at her. She'd had a shower and had changed back into her work clothes. She looked fresh-faced and young. Too young to be running around with vagrants and villains.

"On a side street a ways off from Jackson Square. Kind of hidden. I used to walk through the Quarter every morning. I'd grab a cup of coffee at Café du Monde, maybe an order of beignets. I loved waking up in this city."

"You're speaking in past tense," Josie replied. "Don't you still love New Orleans?"

"I do." He turned to face her so she'd see the sincerity in his eyes. "But I don't love the corruption at every corner, the gangsters and criminals that feed on desperate people."

Josie's cat eyes flared to a brilliant simmer. "Is that what happened to you?"

"Yes." He'd never admitted that to anyone else. "My mother's life was a facade. I understand that facade now. She was young and single and scared. She had two children by two different men. She worked hard to provide for us, but she forgot to be there with us and she forgot that we both had fathers we'd never know. The more successful she became, the less of a mother she turned out to be. She got caught up in status and appearances, but she checked out on maintaining a budget or a relationship with her children."

He watched a tugboat moving toward a flat barge piled high with cartons of goods. "I don't think she ever got over my father, and she didn't love Deidre's father. After she died and we realized we were broke, I did things . . . to survive . . . and to protect Deidre."

"Deidre went to one of the best schools in the U.K.," Josie said. "I saw that in your file."

"And did you also see that I dropped out of high school and . . . got into a whole lot of trouble?"

She nodded, watched the ferry crossing the river. "But you also went on to get your GED and a college education—through determination and with con money. I read everything, Connor. Before I came here, I was briefed, since I knew I'd be your handler. I kept asking myself 'Who is this man? Who is Connor Randall?' I didn't even know if that was your real name or an alias."

"My real name is Randall Connor." He shrugged. "I turned it around to make it more mysterious. Did it work?"

She laughed, her smile hitting at that spot inside his heart that tightened each time he thought about her. "I think it did. You are a mystery. Bad guy turned good. Or still a con man? I can't be sure."

Connor stared across at her, then reached up to touch her still-damp hair. "We've been together for close to forty-eight hours now, and you still don't trust me?"

"I trust you," she said, her eyes wide and clear. "I just don't know what to do about you."

"What's there to do?" he asked, his fingers curled in her hair. "Except your job."

"I'm not talking about my job," she said on a husky whisper.

"Oh." He leaned in, took in the spicy scent of the hotel shampoo she'd used on her hair. "Then you must be talking about this."

The kiss was broad and sweeping, like a painter stroking a fresh canvas. Connor savored each touch, each sigh, each spark of awareness. He tugged her closer, the feel of her in his arms too strong to resist. All of those sensations he'd felt since the day he'd met her came bubbling to the surface like lost treasure. Like lost hope.

Josie tugged away, shaking her head. She caught her breath. "We shouldn't be doing this." Her eyes said differently.

"We shouldn't be on the run from killers, either," he countered. "A lot can happen, Josie. My mother died in an instant and I never even told her how sorry I was for the things I said and did because I blamed her for too many things. Your dad went to prison in an instant, after conning people out of their money for years."

"So that makes this right?" she asked, stepping away. "Just because we're forced together and we feel exposed and justified?"

"No, this is the only right thing in our lives now, right now. This is a different kind of exposure, the kind where two people learn to adjust and trust each other. And maybe to just go with our feelings. What's so wrong with that?"

"Everything," she said, shaking her head. "I'm supposed to watch you, watch out for you and make sure you don't walk away from your obligations."

"I don't plan to walk away," he replied, a silent rage draining him of any hope. When would someone finally see that about him? When would she see the real him? "And I've stopped running. You need to understand that."

"And you need to understand that my job has to come first. I won't be a conquest, Connor. I can't."

"But . . . you want to be with me," he replied. "I know a kiss when I feel it. That was a good kiss."

"Yes, the kiss felt good," she admitted. "But the consequences won't feel so great. And that's what we both need to remember."

A commotion in the hallway stopped them both in their tracks.

"We also need to remember that we're still on somebody's hit list," she said on a hiss of a whisper. Then, without a backward glance, she went for her weapon and went back to work.

TEN . . .

Connor rushed to the door and peered through the keyhole.

"Looks like a bellhop passing by with a cart of suitcases."

Josie breathed a sigh of relief. That kiss had left her so rattled and shaken, she felt like a jigsaw puzzle. That kind of notion could get her in serious trouble.

He turned to stare over at her. "Are we okay here, Josie?"

Josie didn't think she'd be okay for a while to come. "I don't know," she said, aiming for sarcasm. "I mean, since we're been thrown together I've gone undercover, gotten way too close to a Mafia boss and the bomb waiting to kill him, lost someone on my FBI team and I've been shot at several times." She paced around the hotel room, wondering what to do next. "Of course, I've also had some of the best food in the world at the Crooked Nail and I've slept in a boathouse and had a firsthand tour of a swamp." She shrugged. "Oh, and I've been kissed by the elusive Connor Randall. Yeah, sure, I'm A-OK."

"Very funny." He marched toward her with a predatory stare, then took her back in his arms. "One more kiss for the road, then I'll behave until we're done with all this mess."

Josie tried to back away, but Connor swooped in and held her in an embrace so he could do a repeat of their first kiss. She tried to move but her legs locked on her. The only thing she could do was sigh and go with it.

Until they heard someone tapping at the door.

Connor pulled away and put a finger to his lips.

She nodded, got her head together and made sure her weapon was secure. "Hold back and see what happens."

Connor glanced around. "The door to the adjoining room is locked. No escape unless you want to rappel eight floors down."

"Not on my bucket list," she replied. His room was across the hall, but that wouldn't help them now. "Let's give them the element of surprise."

Connor quickly unplugged a lamp and moved toward the door. "I'll surprise 'em all right."

The intruder stopped knocking but Josie heard a click. A key card? She waited in the bathroom while Connor positioned himself around the corner by a small love seat.

The door slid open in a slow creak. Josie waited

just long enough to get her foot against the door. "Hold it right there."

Connor didn't wait. He came barreling around the corner and rammed the upended lamp right toward the startled man standing there with his mouth open.

The lamp made contact and the big man went down and moaned. "It's me. It's me."

"Beaux?" Josie still held her gun high, but she took her foot off the door and helped Connor pull the man into the room. "What do you think you're doing?"

Connor was inches away, but he let go of his grip on the lamp and took a deep breath. "Why are you breaking into this room?"

Beaux held up his beefy hands. "I had to come. Mr. Armond is awake but he's pretending to not be awake. They've moved him, but I got to him in the hospital and he wanted me to find y'all and warn you."

"What?" Josie shot a glance toward Connor. "Get in here, Beaux. And don't make me regret letting you live."

Beaux clomped toward the sofa and plopped down, his beefy hand on his head. He was sweating and nervous. "I didn't know what else to do. I followed y'all and I bribed a bellman to give me a master key. And I'm trying to be discreet."

As discreet as a burly giant of a man could be, Josie decided. And he was lying. "Beaux, that dog won't hunt. What are you talking about?"

Beaux's big eyes widened. "What do you mean?"

"How did you find us?" Connor asked.

"The FBI has been after all of us," Beaux explained. "They keep waiting for Mr. A. to wake up. He's in and out but he's playing possum on talking. He knows they found something out at the house and he believes he's been set up. He's afraid the killer will come back, too."

"What happened in that room at the other hotel?" Josie asked.

Beaux shrugged. "We had a knock at the door, and I thought it was the guard you told me was coming. When I opened the door, the guard showed me a badge and a gun and told me to take a break. So I went down to the cafeteria, but something didn't feel right. When I got back, all sorts of people were in the hallway, so I hid near the ice machine."

"They were there to take Mr. Armond into custody," Connor explained. "What happened after that?"

"Before I could warn Mr. Armond, another group of men came in and started shooting. I hung back and watched. They shot up the place." He showed them a cut on the side of his head. "When things quieted down, I hurried back, but everyone was gone and I . . . I thought Mr. A. was dead. I ain't proud, but I bolted when I heard someone else coming."

Sherwood had told Josie that Beaux had gotten away.

"So you've been in hiding since?"

"Yes." He rubbed his head. "I watched and waited and disguised myself, then I finally asked around and found where they were holding Mr. A. in a private room at that big hospital near the Garden District. I only got to see him for a couple of minutes. He warned me to get away." He rubbed his head. "I saw them taking him out of the hospital, but I don't know what they did with him. I had to stay out of sight so I could find y'all."

"Is he afraid to talk?" Josie asked, handing Beaux a glass of water.

"He's afraid of breathing," Beaux replied. "We got the FBI trailing us and somebody trying to off all of us."

"Is Armond's empire crumbling?" Connor asked.

"Yes, it is," Beaux said. "I . . . I listened in when the FBI was talking nearby his room." He gave Josie a hard stare. "I know you're FBI but I ain't gonna tell anyone. I didn't even tell Mr. Armond. All I know is you tried to help him and then, boom, someone shot him. I saw y'all after all the fireworks in that other hotel. I shoulda stayed there and helped Mr. A., but I panicked."

Connor let out a groan. "Did you tail us, Beaux?"

"Nah, not since y'all left town. I been holed up at a run-down hotel out on the interstate. That's the truth. But I knew if I hung around the Quarter long enough, I'd probably see somebody who could help me. The FBI and those other agencies took all of Mr. A.'s files, computers—you name it, they stripped it. They want to pin Lewanna's shooting on him, and they think they've got some other evidence or something. But they don't have any proof of nothing on the shooting, 'cause they can't find the weapon. They swept that mansion clean."

He inhaled a deep breath, then let it out.

"I got to stay close or I'll be a fugitive. Only I don't have anywhere to stay, since Mr. Armond is so sick. I ain't going back to that house. I don't like that place. His wife won't even come back to check on him. She's scared. Gone into hiding."

"Interesting," Connor said, shooting Josie a glance. "So why did you come to us?"

Beaux leaned in and lowered his voice. "Mr. Armond whispered something in my ear before he fell back asleep."

"What did he say?" Josie asked, her patience about to crack.

"He told me to find Randall and . . . that broad." He glanced at Josie. "Sorry, his word, not mine."

Josie did an eye roll. "It's okay, Beaux. What do you want us to do?"

Beaux swallowed some water. "Mr. Armond

might still be mad at you, Connor. He says if he ever leaves that hospital alive, he has to find you."

"So he sent you here as a courtesy, to warn us?" Connor asked.

Beaux shook his head. "He was confused and forgetful, but he didn't tell me to kill you. Besides, I like you, Connor. And . . . I ain't got no beef with you, FBI lady."

Josie would never understand the criminal mind. This man was obviously a gentle giant, but he'd gotten himself caught up in a world of crime. He did as he was told as long as he had a safe place to stay and a gun to protect him.

She touched Beaux on the shoulder. "Did you cut a deal with Armond? Or maybe you need to talk to the FBI?"

"Maybe," Beaux replied, his eyes misty.

"It's okay," Connor said. "I sealed my fate by agreeing to work with the FBI. I don't blame you for doing the same."

"I haven't done anything yet," Beaux said, perspiration pooling in big drops on his brow. "I don't want to work with them, 'cause if Mr. A, finds out, I'm toast. So I came to warn y'all." He shrugged. "I'm mostly wanting to find out why Mr. A. told me to go back to the big house and secure the garage."

"The garage," Josie and Connor said at the same time.

Beaux bobbed his head. "He kept whispering

about a car in the garage. Maybe his Bentley?"

"What is it about that garage?" Josie asked out loud. "Something's in there. Which means we need to get back out to that house before someone else does."

Connor rubbed his forehead and started in on Beaux again. "So we've got someone on our tail trying to blast us, and now we've got a new message from Armond, but you don't want to go back out to the house, so . . . again, what do you want from us?"

Beaux got up and shook out his wrinkled suit. "I want you both to run as far from Louisiana as you can get. Don't go back to that house. It's the only way to keep you alive."

"Does the FBI know you're here?"

Beaux shook his head at Connor's question. "No, but I'm hoping they'll cut me some slack if I help y'all get away. Maybe y'all could vouch for me. I got a family to consider."

Josie wished he'd considered his family before selling his soul to a bunch of criminals.

"Do you know who's after Armond?" Josie asked.

Beaux stood there, as if weighing his next words very carefully. "I have my suspicions."

"And?"

"I'm thinking Mrs. A. went to New York to hire someone to do away with Mr. A., starting with that troublemaker Lewanna."

"His wife?" Josie shot a questioning glance at Connor, then looked back at Beaux. "Do you have any proof?"

"She hates him fiercely," Beaux said on a low whisper.

"Motive," Connor pointed out.

"And the means?" Josie asked.

"The son, Lou, was in the military for a little while," Beaux said. "He got kicked out for disobeying orders. It wasn't pretty. They tried to hide it. Sent him to Europe. But he's still causing a stink, always gambling and asking for money." Beaux lowered his voice. "He likes to blow things up."

"Surprise, surprise," Connor quipped. "So you think mother and son have teamed up to off Mr. Armond?"

Beaux nodded. "Mr. A. thinks so, too. But you see, they say he has another son hidden away somewhere."

Another revelation. Connor got up to pace but he didn't seem surprised. Had he heard this, too?

His next question indicated he hadn't. "You mean Lou isn't Louis Armond's only son?"

"Nope, or so they say. I heard Mr. and Mrs. A. arguing about it one night long ago. Never forgot that fight, let me tell you. Throwing stuff and slamming doors."

"Does his wife hate Armond enough to have him killed?" Connor said on a dry note.

"I think so," Beaux replied. "She mighta found out the will don't leave very much for Lou."

"Lou, the firstborn?" Josie couldn't believe these new revelations.

"That's the problem. He might not be the firstborn."

"But if he kills his father and no one knows about the other son, he could stand to inherit a lot of money through dear old mom."

"Exactly," Beaux agreed. "And his mama could team up with whoever it is that's supposed to be a silent partner. Somebody hugely powerful, is all I know. I've never seen Mr. A. scared before."

"Maybe the proof is somewhere on the estate," Connor said. "That garage has all kinds of storage places and hidden cubbyholes. Maybe even another safe. Or maybe the old garage."

Beaux turned stubborn. "I ain't going out there to find anything."

"Beaux, do you know anything at all about this silent partner?" Josie asked. "Or the other son?"

Beaux's eyes widened. "No. Not a thing." Then he lowered his head. "Okay, maybe. But Mr. A. don't confide in me about those kinds of deals."

Connor and Josie exchanged glances. Josie figured Beaux knew too much but he was afraid to talk now.

"I need y'all to find whoever is doing this," Beaux said. "They'll kill all of us if the FBI doesn't get to us first." He wiped his brow. "I need y'all alive. And I plan to stay that way, too."

"Why are you warning us like this?" Josie asked, her mind trying to comprehend this turn of events.

"Mr. A. told me," Beaux said. "He didn't make a whole lot of sense 'cause he's so mad and scared." He gave Connor a solemn stare. "But he told me himself—said to protect Connor. Warn Connor Randall. Remind him of the garage. I think you need to find out what he's talking about."

"Good point." Connor looked over at Josie. "What do you want to do?"

"I'm not running," she said. "I'd like to get to Lou and Vanessa Armond and check out Beaux's suspicions."

Connor got up and slapped Beaux on the back. "You heard the lady. We'll take care of this. But first, we need a favor from you."

"What's that?" Beaux asked.

Josie stood, too. "We need you to get us back inside Armond Gardens. Tonight. We think we can find some answers out there."

"I told you I didn't want to go back there," Beaux said, "but you'd better let your boss know about this, 'cause there ain't much left to search. They had warrants and papers and a whole slew of law-enforcement people out there this morning. Saw that on the news. The whole mess is on the front page of the paper, too. So you need to leave my name out of this. I'm already in enough trouble."

"I'll get Sherwood on the phone right now and get clearance," Josie said, already holding her phone to her ear. "And as for you, Beaux, you need to stick with us. But we'll protect you, so we never had this conversation."

Midnight in Armond Gardens.

Connor could smell the danger. The hot air was tinged with heat lightning and dark clouds. A storm. Just what they needed.

Beaux had smuggled them into a sleek black SUV and moved them through the city while they huddled down in the far backseat. Then they'd taken the back roads north toward the Old River Road and the back gate to the Armond estate.

And with each bump and bang on the rough roads and unpaved trails, he'd been so close to Josie he could feel her heart beating. He remembered kissing her, remembered the fresh new feelings washing over him with that kiss.

She'd returned it, measure for measure. The woman had a thing for him. He could feel it. Could they make a good team?

She shifted now. "Are we there yet?"

"Almost. It takes longer coming the back way."

"I'm getting mighty tired of these Louisiana back roads."

"But our lovely vacation is just starting, sweet-heart."

"Funny. Shut up."

He grabbed her hand. "If I have to be on the run, I'm glad it's with you."

"You might change your tune on that," she whispered. "I'm not in a good mood."

One more bounce and the SUV rocked to a sudden halt.

"Beaux, what's wrong?"

"We got trouble," Beaux said, his words rushed.

"What now?" Josie lifted her head, then let out a groan. "We're too late, Connor."

Connor raised his head. "What's going on?"

"I can't go any farther," Beaux replied. "See? Up ahead."

Connor saw the bright orange blaze. "Is the house on fire?"

"I think so," Beaux said. "And if it is, we need to be away from this place."

"No." Josie stretched and launched herself between the captain seats. "No. We need to investigate."

Connor knew he wouldn't be able to stop her, but he tried. "Josie, Beaux's right. We can't be caught here."

"I'm going." She was already opening a door. "And I'm calling it in. I should have stayed here the other night and I didn't. Tonight, I'm doing my job."

Connor groaned and climbed out after her. "Beaux, stay here and don't make a move. If we're not back in an hour, come looking for us."

Beaux nodded. "Be careful."

Connor saw the irony of a hit man telling them to be careful while they headed toward a raging fire at a Mafia don's big estate. Yeah, they'd be real careful.

By the time they'd trekked up the back part of the vast property, they could already hear sirens off in the distance.

"The village volunteers," he said, halting Josie a few yards from the big house.

"Look," she said. "It's not the house. It's the garage."

Connor squinted into the bright flames. "The six-car garage behind the house. The very place we're here to search. The place where my car used to be."

"That'd be the one. At least your car is probably safe back in the city."

He could see it now. The garage was directly behind the house but about fifty yards away. From where they'd stopped earlier, it had looked like the mansion was on fire.

"Why would someone set fire to the garage?" Josie asked, her tone full of sarcasm.

"They hate black SUVs?"

"Or they knew something was in that garage. Something no one was supposed to see. The same something Armond warned Beaux about."

He turned from the flames to Josie. "Now what?"

"We can wait 'em out and investigate later but this fire might destroy any evidence we could use."

"You know the feds will be all over this," he reminded her. "Wait, you are a fed."

"Yes, and I need to let Sherwood know that we're on the scene. He won't like that we came out here on our own, but that's a perfect excuse for investigating this fire, too."

"But, Josie, whoever set this fire might still be around. Maybe they set it to lure us out here."

Her chin lifted. "Or as a distraction."

"So they could go into the main house and get whatever it is they don't want anyone to find," Connor finished.

"Exactly. Let's get moving."

He had to follow her. He didn't have any other choice.

He wanted to solve this mystery and get out from under this hit so he could enjoy being with Josie in a more relaxed, normal situation.

But could he actually spend his life with an FBI agent?

"I guess this is a good practice run," he mumbled as he hurried to catch up with her. "If we survive this, we can survive anything."

ELEVEN . . .

They jogged along the fence line and stayed in the shadows near the oak shrubs and tall grasses.

"Tell me again why we need to do this?" Connor asked, his hand on Josie's elbow as they rushed toward the scene. He was halfway teasing but he wanted to talk this through one more time.

"We have to do a thorough search of the house and outbuildings, especially that burning garage. Except now we have to make sure no one is hurt or in danger from that fire."

Connor thought of all the rules her supervisor, Sherwood, had allowed them to break. He found that odd. "Does it bother you that your boss has given you so much freedom?"

Her frown was shadowed in moonlight. "Why should it? He expects me to investigate Armond, and I'm doing that while I also try to keep you alive. He's got Armond. Now he just needs more evidence to hold him. He's got the alleged shooting of the mistress, but with no concrete witnesses and no weapon to prove it, that can only hold up for so long." She shrugged. "The money can be explained away and those invoices have to be validated. In the meantime,

I'd like to stay alive and get back to my other cases."

Connor clapped his hands. "You actually make sense."

"Look," she said, waving her right hand toward the fire. "The garage is on fire but help is coming. It's empty, right? We confiscated all the vehicles."

"Right." Connor glanced at the big stucco garage. "But some of the lowly employees did have rooms up there."

Josie whirled to stare at him. "Are you saying someone could be trapped in that garage?"

"I'm saying people had rooms there," Connor replied. "But they're either in custody or out of the country by now."

"We have to check it out."

Josie took off running, leaving him in the dust again.

Wishing she'd quit doing that, Connor followed her, his mind whirling with how to spin this explanation in case they got in trouble.

She's an FBI agent. That gives her jurisdiction, and the earlier interview with Big Beaux, along with what they found in the safe, gives her probable cause to enter and search the premises. And the fire is an emergency situation, so that gets first dibs.

Why was he so worried about rules and regulations now?

Because he was worried about Josie.

That also made perfect sense.

Didn't it?

He shouted after her, "Josie, be careful."

Connor reached her just as one end of the garage caved in. He grabbed her and pulled her around. "We can't go in there."

She held up a hand to shield her face from the heat. "What if someone is trapped?"

He heard the sirens growing closer. "The fire department will verify that. This place will soon be running over with the usual law-enforcement people. If we want to stay undercover, we might want to stay hidden, remember?"

She glanced from him to the road. "The gate? How will they get in?" She pushed at her hair. "We can't stand by now. We have to help the firemen."

"I know the code," Connor replied, already running toward the house. "You stay here and update them. I'll be back soon."

"Okay." She seemed to move closer to the fire as he ran away.

"Don't do anything crazy!" he called over his shoulder.

But his plea got lost in the wind and now the rain.

Josie squinted into the white-hot flames, the smell of electrical wires and burning wood and plastic making her cough. She'd have to get away before this place blew up.

The raindrops hit her with a wet frenzy, and she thanked God for them. "Yes. Stop the fire. Please, stop this fire."

Who had done this and why? Did someone hate Armond so much that they wanted to destroy him completely? Or was someone trying to destroy important documents? More invoices with even more damaging information? Or a whole cache of illegal goods? Maybe even the coveted will?

Or was someone after Connor? Maybe only Connor? He had fooled and betrayed a lot of people before he turned FBI asset. Maybe she should consider that angle, too.

She heard a crackle and then another part of the roof fell in. She turned to run but a scream turned her back toward the fire.

Somebody was in there.

Connor let in the lone fire truck and told the volunteer fire chief where the fire was located. "You should see a dark-headed female back there," he shouted. Then he hopped up onto the big truck's bumper and rode with them. "I'll show you."

But when the truck got closer, the rain hit, washing him with a cold, fresh rinse. He wiped at his eyes as the sharp drops hit him in the face. He didn't see Josie anywhere.

She'd disappeared on him again, and once again his heart did that tightening thing that made him want to scream. He wasn't sure he was ready to care about a woman who was so fearless, but his heart wasn't listening to his head.

"Where's the woman?" one of the volunteers shouted.

"I left her here," Connor shouted back. He hopped off the truck and ran toward the growing flames. "Josie?"

Lightning flared across the sky, beaming across the burning garage. Connor squinted into the bright light while the firemen went to work with the pumper truck. He hurried closer to the big building but the extreme heat burned at his skin. A roaring, raging sound filled the night. The fire taking over, moving rapidly across the entire building.

"Josie?"

Had she gone in there?

Josie held her arm across her mouth and nose and searched the yellow-hot building, her eyes burning from the heat. "Hello? Anyone in here?"

She heard a muffled call. "Over here. Help me, please."

Josie followed the sound, smoke clouding her in a scorching blanket of choking heat. "Keep calling," she shouted. "I'm coming."

She heard a woman's whimpering plea. "Hurry."

Josie was almost to the back of the garage but

the flames were licking hungrily all around her. Taking off her jacket, she pushed it against her nose. "Where are you?"

"Here, here." A tiny dark-haired woman appeared out of the smoke. "Help me."

Josie rushed toward the woman, but when she heard timber cracking behind her, she turned and looked up toward the stairs leading to the apartments. The fire was headed that way. In a brief flash, she thought she saw a man standing at the top of the stairs. She blinked to clear her eyes, but no one was there. Then the woman screamed, closer this time, and Josie turned back toward her.

"Hurry," she called. "Follow me out."

The woman looked terrified. "I won't make it."

"Yes, you will."

All around them, wood was splitting and popping, while ribbons of smoke poured over them like liquid silver. Josie turned to grab the woman but then she heard the high beams of the big building buckling into the flames like matchsticks.

She looked up and instinctively held her hand over her head and watched in horror as one of the beams creaked and moaned. Without thinking, she lunged toward the woman and threw her body over her.

The beam hit the garage floor with a crashing collapse right in the place where Josie had been standing.

She lifted her head to make sure the woman was all right and then saw the flames lapping at them like fire water.

There was no way out.

Connor shouted to the firemen, "She's in there. Josie! She's inside."

"Get back and let us do our job," one of the men shouted.

But Connor couldn't stand there. Searching the building, he saw an open door, and before anyone could stop him, he ran with all his might into the fire. He had to find Josie.

Once inside, he held his head against his arm, lifting it away to call out, "Josie? Josie, where are you?"

No answer.

He couldn't give up. Why had she come in here?

And how was he going to get her and himself out alive?

"Hurry," Josie called, holding the woman behind her as they stepped over fallen metal shelves and boxes of old auto parts. Bruised and cut, Josie coughed with each breath. The woman echoed that same cough. They needed fresh air.

She'd found a small corner where the fire hadn't crossed the concrete floor yet. She thought she saw another side door back there, but she could be wrong.

The roof above them groaned with the weight of burned beams and now heavy rain. At least the rain was doing its best to subdue the roaring flames. She couldn't be sure but she thought she'd heard the stairs crumbling.

"C'mon," she said, urging the woman toward the door. "We have to hurry. If the wind shifts, the flames will leap over into this area and we'll be trapped."

"I can't." The older woman had dark hair and black eyes. She was dressed in what had been an expensive white pantsuit, which was now smeared with dirt and soot. "I can't. Too tired."

Josie turned to the hysterical woman and shouted over the rain and wind, "You need to get out of here or you'll die. We'll both die." With that, she tightened her grip on the petite woman and practically lifted her up and over the final two feet toward the side door. She prayed it wasn't locked. Or blocked.

"No, no!" The woman's frantic shouts filled the air as she tried to twist away. "I have to go back inside."

"Let's go! Now!" Josie's breath was caught in a web of hot, choking smoke and her head burned with a pulsating heat. Would she have to knock this little spitfire out to save her?

Before she resorted to that, two strong hands grabbed the fighting woman and lifted her up into the air.

Connor.

"Are you all right?" he called to Josie.

She nodded and pointed toward the beckoning door, flames chasing her even though the rain was still pouring.

Connor followed, dragging the frantic woman with him.

Josie called to him, "When I open this door, it might suck the flames toward us. We have to run."

He nodded, both hands on the scared woman.

With a grunt and a tug, Josie took her coat and grabbed at the door handle. It flew open with a whine and she ran through it, welcoming the cold, wet rain while the scalding heat burst in a trail, chasing behind her. She turned to make sure Connor had the woman and saw him emerging right behind her.

Within seconds, they went from hot and ash-covered to wet and shivering, but they'd saved the mysterious woman.

And once again, Connor had saved Josie.

A few minutes later, the little lady stared up at Connor, her scowl full of recognition. Between inhales of oxygen and coughing, she shouted, "You! This is all your fault."

A fireman came up and took over, insisting the woman should be checked out at the nearby ambulance. But she was still kicking and pointing a finger at Connor.

"Who is she?" Josie asked, her shock followed by realization after she heard his intake of breath. Then she figured it out. "Vanessa Armond? Connor, is this Armond's wife?"

Connor bobbed his head, his hands moving over Josie's wet, smut-smeared face. "I'm not worried about her right now. Are you all right?"

"I'm fine." Josie pushed away the oxygen mask a paramedic tried to keep on her. Still coughing, she kept talking while the medic checked her airway. "I heard her screaming. She wanted something and she obviously thought it was in that garage. She didn't want to come with me."

Connor's gaze hit on the mad little woman, who was now shouting at the top of her lungs to the paramedic team and the sheriff deputy. He took the mask and forced it over Josie's hair and down on her face. "Breathe into this, Josie." After she did as he told her, he asked, "Think she set the fire?"

"I haven't had a chance to question her." Josie got up and handed the oxygen mask to the frustrated paramedic and then hurried to where the woman sat on the back of the ambulance with a blanket around her.

Vanessa Armond didn't want to be checked over, either, but the paramedic did his job. "Your nose hairs aren't singed. No smoke inhalation that I can tell, but you need to be checked out at a hospital."

"No hospital," Vanessa said, daring anyone to dispute her. "I'm okay. I . . . I only ran in because of the fire." She gave Josie a heated glare. "I needed to find something, but she forced me out." Vanessa's dark eyes moved from Connor to Josie. "Who did you bring into my home?"

Giving up on staying undercover, Josie flashed her badge at the deputy and then made sure Mrs. Armond saw it, too. The deputy nodded and hurried over to report to the sheriff.

"FBI?" Vanessa Armond almost spat the question. "Where is my husband? Where is Louis?"

"He's safe for now," Josie said. "He's injured—he got shot—but we have him in protective custody, since he's had two attempts on his life."

The woman turned her wrath on Connor. "This is on you. You and your charming ways. I told Louis not to trust you."

Connor replied calmly, "He doesn't really trust anybody, including you."

Vanessa lifted up to go for Connor, but Josie interceded. "Just for the record, are you Vanessa Armond?"

"Yes, I am," the woman replied, her accent heavy. "Thank you for saving my life, but I will not talk to you any further."

She tried to stand but she started to wobble again. Connor grabbed her and turned to the paramedic. "I'm taking her inside. She lives here. If anyone needs to question her or get our statements, you can find us inside the main house."

The young paramedic looked at Vanessa. "Are you sure, ma'am? You need to be checked over at a hospital."

"I'm fine now, thank you." Vanessa nodded to Connor while she signed some paperwork. Then she turned back to the first responders. "Thank you all so much. If I don't feel any better, I'll go to a hospital."

The fire chief walked up. "We'll need to question you later, ma'am. Don't leave the premises." He shot Josie a measured glance. "Keep an eye on her for now. We think this fire was set intentionally."

"I don't intend to go anywhere," Vanessa Armond snapped.

Connor and Josie helped her toward the big, dark house.

When they were safely inside, Vanessa Armond turned to Connor with wide, worried eyes. "What happened here? I came home to police tape and a burned bed. Where is my husband?"

Josie brought the tray of coffee and water over to the big wooden table across from the kitchen counter and placed it in front of Mrs. Armond. Connor had found pain pills and crackers.

"You need to drink this water," he told Mrs. Armond.

After pouring them all some of the strong

coffee, Josie sat down next to the fierce little woman. "As I already told you, he's safe. He's being guarded. But I have to explain to you, when he wakes up he will be questioned regarding the death of Lewanna Munford. And we've collected some incriminating evidence that he needs to explain, too."

Vanessa said something in Italian that Josie could only interpret as derogatory toward the dearly departed Lewanna. "She knew to stay away. That was our agreement. I don't know about any evidence, but I do know that woman was supposed to stay out of my way."

"You had an agreement with Lewanna?" Josie asked.

"I did." Vanessa took a sip of her water. "I told her as long as she stayed out of the public eye and stayed away from my son and me, I would pay her a monthly allowance."

Connor shook his head, then glanced over at Vanessa in disbelief. "You paid your husband's mistress?"

"To stay out of my way and to be discreet, yes."

"Did you kill Lewanna?" Josie asked, trying to read the woman's body language and mood.

"No, no." Vanessa started crying. "I didn't do that. I've been in New York visiting my sick mother." She glared at Connor, obviously daring him to dispute her.

Josie wondered if her explanation was code

for taking care of business. "And how is your mother?"

Vanessa's dark eyes boiled with rage. "She's in a retirement home."

"I see. And I can get verification that you were with her over the last few days?"

"Yes." Vanessa turned to Connor with a lethal glare. "You bring this into my home, after all Louis did for you?"

Josie had planned to get to this part, so she waited to see how Connor would handle Vanessa Armond's accusations.

"I didn't bring this," Connor replied, his tone sure and firm. "Your husband did. But someone set him up. They killed Lewanna to scare him and then they tried to blow him up in his own bed. Then they came after him and shot him." He hesitated, then added, "I believe someone planted that evidence."

"What kind of evidence?" Vanessa asked.

"We aren't at liberty to say," Josie replied, giving Connor a warning glance. For all they knew, Vanessa could have set up her husband.

Vanessa shuddered and started praying in Italian. "I tried to warn him. I tried to stop this. He never listens to me and now he's ruined everything."

"Stop what?" Josie asked, still curious as to what Vanessa had been looking for out in the garage.

As if realizing she'd said something she shouldn't have, Vanessa clammed up. "I want my lawyer."

"Why do you need a lawyer?" Connor asked.

"I won't tell you. And I won't tell her."

"Our suspect has turned hostile," Josie replied. "Time to call in my immediate superior." She brought out her phone. "Of course, he'll have to question you at the FBI headquarters in town, and you know how the newshounds hang around, just waiting for a big story like this."

"Stop," Vanessa said, her finger in the air.

Connor took that as his cue, his nod toward Josie telling her he could make this work. "Vanessa, I know you think I betrayed Louis, but I didn't. I didn't give the FBI anything on him last year because I never found anything. I found the Benoit paintings, and that's all I did. He proved they belonged in his family, and he did the right thing by allowing them to be put on tour."

He leaned toward her. "Neither you nor I gave up anything else to the FBI. But I've been watching your husband for some time now, hoping to get him into protective custody. He's scared now, but before all of this happened he'd agreed to talk to me. But someone scared him off. And because of my association with him, someone wants me dead now."

"He should have killed you that night last year,"

Vanessa said, anger turning her pale skin pink. "You. He's always favored you over the others."

"What does that mean?" Josie asked, hoping the woman would slip up and give them a clue.

"Nothing." Vanessa's fiery gaze stayed on Connor. "Louis has a lot of people doing his bidding, but this one—what my husband saw in him I'll never know. He didn't even have the guts to get rid of this con man when he had the chance."

Josie shot Connor a questioning glance. "You do have the gift of persuasion on your side."

"He has a lot more than that going for him," Vanessa shouted. "Now he's accusing Louis of cooperating with the feds. Ha, that will never happen. And making up stories of Louis wanting to tell secrets. Nonsense."

"Let's get back to the paintings," Josie said. "Do you think someone is after them?"

Vanessa waved her bejeweled fingers in the air. "Those paintings are paltry compared to our real money," she said on a smug breath. "And if you think this is all because you hung around here snooping, then you are deadly wrong."

"Care to elaborate?" Josie retorted. "Is that why you were in the garage? To find something valuable? Or did you set the fire to hide some incriminating activities?"

"No." Vanessa glanced back to the embers of the garage. "But I . . . I need to go back out to the garage. I had something stored out there. Very important papers."

Josie leaned close. "Such as?"

"Such as none of your business," Vanessa replied. "I want my lawyer."

"Give us a minute," Connor said. He got up and motioned Josie over to the kitchen sink. "I might be able to convince her to share," he said. "I know a few things about her, too."

"And you'll use that against her?"

"If I need to."

"What do you know?" She wondered if he'd been playing her, telling her he'd never found enough to help put Armond away.

"We both know something we can use as leverage. Remember what Beaux told us?"

"Right." Josie stared over at Vanessa Armond. "It's worth a try." Then she whirled back to Connor. "Speaking of Beaux, have you seen him since we left him out on the road?"

"No." Connor glanced outside, his phone already to his ear. "He's not answering. I'll go check on things and try to find him."

"Don't be gone too long," Josie replied. "Meanwhile, I'll get back to the lady of the house."

Connor headed out, leaving Josie with Mrs. Armond.

"How's Lou?" Josie asked to test the waters.

Vanessa's head shot up. "What do you mean?"

Josie tapped her fingers on the table. "I mean how is your son doing?"

"You stay away from my boy."

The look in Vanessa's dark eyes should have scared Josie, but instead it gave her an adrenaline rush. For the first time since this whole weird episode had started, she'd found a weak spot in the Armond armor. This mother would do anything to protect her only child, even if it meant breaking the law. Josie's father had tried to protect his family from his crimes, but in the end, his house of cards had caught up with him. And their family had crumbled.

The same thing was happening to the Armonds. She should feel sorry for this woman, but she couldn't find it in her heart to forgive just yet.

"I'm not going to harm your son, Mrs. Armond. But you both might be in danger. Someone is out to kill your entire family. Your husband is in and out of consciousness and being guarded by the police and the FBI, and you're scared about something that might have burned up in your garage. What about your son, Lou? Are you sure he's safe?"

Vanessa jumped up and started pulling at her blanket. "I have to talk to Louis. You need to take me to see my husband, right now."

"I'll do that," Josie said, getting up, too. "I think that's a very good idea."

She buzzed Connor. When he didn't answer,

155

she texted him. We need to take her to see her husband.

"Let's go," Vanessa said. "Now."

"I have to wait for Connor and Big Beaux," Josie said. "They should be here in a few minutes."

But after ten minutes and still no sign of Connor, Josie got worried. "Are you able to walk?" she asked Vanessa.

"I'm fine."

"Then we're going to find Connor."

She took Vanessa by the arm. "And please, don't try anything, Mrs. Armond. I do have my weapon."

"And so do I," said the man standing at the open back door.

Josie held Mrs. Armond behind her but not for long. The woman gasped and rushed around her. "Lou."

"It's me, Mom," the dark-haired man said. "And I found these two snooping around outside."

He pushed Connor and Big Beaux inside and shut the door.

"Now, together, I think we can get to the bottom of things," he said, waving his semiautomatic in the air. "Because nobody's leaving here until we do."

TWELVE . . .

Vanessa Armond hugged her son, her Italian greeting swift and hard to interpret.

Connor focused on Josie, hoping to convey that now wouldn't be a good time to become a hero. She had her hand on her waistband, obviously going for her gun. But Lou Armond was a mean, ruthless son of a criminal who had the dark playboy looks that belied his cold personality. Right now, Lou's black eyes held a cruel intent. He'd waylaid Beaux and held him in the dark until someone convenient came along.

Connor had been that someone. Ambushed and now trapped, because Junior had made it clear he'd shoot Josie if Connor tried any tricks. Connor wouldn't put it past Lou to set that fire. He had appeared right after they'd arrived, but he'd held Beaux so the authorities didn't find them.

Lou hugged his mother but kept the gun on Connor and Beaux. Then he pointed the gun straight at Connor but his gaze hit on Josie. "Take out your weapon and place it on the floor, or someone might get hurt."

Connor lifted his head toward Josie. "Leave her alone."

She gave him a sharp glance, then trained her eyes on Lou Armond. "You look nothing like your father," she said on a daring note. But she slowly took out her weapon and held the barrel down.

Connor watched as she mirrored Lou's every move. Was she trying to win the man over or get herself killed?

"On the floor," Lou said. "Shove it over here."

She kicked the gun with her booted foot, then glanced back at Connor.

Connor wanted to throw a dish towel at her. She was walking a thin, dangerous line here, trying to mess with a man who had no scruples. What was she up to?

"I take after my mother's side of the family, Agent Gilbert," Lou replied with a touché attitude. He shoved her gun back behind him, near the open French doors out to the patio.

Josie's smile was sugary sweet, but her stance was all business. "Yes, I can see the resemblance."

Vanessa made a throaty sound, but kept watching her son with adoring eyes.

Lou pushed his doting mother out of the way and stalked toward Josie. "What are you and this loser doing on my property?"

"It's your father's property," Josie replied, nose to nose. "We wanted to do a little more investigating, but someone beat us to that. Did you set the garage on fire? I thought I saw someone standing on the second-floor landing in the garage. Was that you?"

Lou shook his head and waved his gun. Motioning for Connor and Beaux to go stand beside Josie, he paced between the heavy wooden breakfast table and the long kitchen counter, his dark gaze hot with anger. "Somebody is messing with my family, and I need to understand who and why. I don't like the FBI sniffing around and I especially don't like this mole nosing around our property."

Connor inclined his head. "I've been called worse, but I wasn't nosing around. Your father mentioned the garage when he woke up from surgery. I owed it to him to come investigate, since he seemed worried about something."

Lou snorted with disdain. "You don't have to investigate anything, since you're just a shadow for the FBI. I should have taken you out a long time ago, Randall."

"Did you get a chance to chat with the fire chief and the police officers also milling around out there?" Josie asked, her tone so calm Connor couldn't help but be impressed. "They're pre-serving the crime scene and bagging evidence—even the tiniest bits of evidence. Your mother has already been checked over. She was inside that burning building."

"They were too busy to notice us," Lou said on

a shrug, but he did glance over his shoulder. "I convinced Beaux to wait in the woods with me. We had such an interesting chat about the weather, politics and, oh, yes, that the FBI had confiscated my father's files and all of the Armond official vehicles."

"He threatened to kill me," Beaux said, his dark eyes bleary and red-rimmed. "Ain't nothing I could do but tell him the truth."

Vanessa grated her words through a clenched jaw. "You're all trespassing. I'm beginning to think one of you started that fire to keep us—"

"Enough, Mother!" Lou pushed his mother into a chair. "The garage isn't a total loss, thanks to the rain and someone calling the ever-alert local volunteers. They've tromped all over the place out there, but we'll deal with that later."

"Lou, please," Vanessa said, her hands trembling in the air. "We need to get out of here. Someone tried to kill me tonight. We have to hurry, darling."

Josie turned to Vanessa. "You never mentioned to us that someone tried to kill you. That's a whole new spin. Did you see someone else in the garage?"

Vanessa looked toward her son, her mouth opening and closing like a clam. "No. No one. Just a feeling."

Lou put a plump finger to his lips. "Shh. The FBI is everywhere and so are their little spies."

He glared at Connor and Josie, hatred darkening his expression. "The big question right now is—what are we to do with these trespassers?"

Josie crossed her arms over her stomach and glared up at him. "I hear you've been out of the country. While your father took care of business."

Lou advanced on her, the glint in his eyes raging like the earlier fire. "You're trying so hard to rattle my chains, but I'm the one holding the gun, remember?"

"I can see that," Josie replied, her gaze sweeping over the stout, dark-haired man. "But you see, you can't do anything to help your father right now. If you tell us what you know, we can help you and your family. We're guarding your father for that very reason."

"Oh, you want me to turn, right?" Lou stomped in a frantic pacing. "You're making up things, wanting me to think my father has agreed to protection from the FBI. That can't happen. I've waited a long time to tell the FBI what it can do with its cameras and listening devices and its petty spies. Now's my chance to do something. I came home to look after my father's interests while he's recovering."

"Or you came home to finish the job," Josie said in disgust. "I'm no fan of Louis Armond's, but even I smell a rat in this room. You've been living off your daddy's money for a long time now. But it's kind of you to be so concerned that you came home to help out, especially since we couldn't locate your mother or you when this happened."

Lou grabbed her by the collar and brought her in front of him. "Hand me her gun," he said to Beaux. With one weapon strapped over his shoulder, he waited for Beaux to hand him the other one.

The other man did as he asked, but Connor couldn't take seeing Josie's gun aimed at her head. He lunged, but Vanessa got in his way, her dainty, dirt-and-smut-covered shoe almost tripping him.

"My mother is very quick for her age, yes?" Lou said. He held Josie's gun to her temple. "Sit down, Mr. Randall, or I will shoot her."

Connor counted to ten and took a seat. He had to stay cool for Josie's sake. "What do you want, Lou? You know you can't escape. The first responders might not have noticed you, but the FBI and the locals will be here all night investigating the fire. They'll move back to the house later, since the master bedroom is still a crime scene. This place will be full of lawmen in a few minutes."

"I know that," Lou replied. "That's why I'm taking her with me."

"No," Beaux and Connor both shouted. But Connor knew it was too late. He could see it in Josie's vivid, on-fire eyes. She wouldn't go with this man because she knew she'd never return.

Josie waited until Lou had her almost out the door, then she looked back at Connor. That look was a call to action. She grunted with all her might, then elbowed Lou Armond, and in a split second, her booted foot rammed into his mid-section.

Lou dropped her gun and went down in a scream of pain. Josie grabbed her weapon, then held it over Lou's face before he could use his gun. "Let go of the rifle."

He grunted and let the rifle drop beside him. Careful to keep her gun on him, Josie swooped down and kicked the rifle well away from his grasp.

Connor grabbed at Lou while Beaux went after Vanessa. Lou's mother was shouting and kicking, but Beaux held on. "I got her," he shouted. Then he growled in her ear, "Hush up, Mrs. A. I ain't gonna hurt you."

Lou let out a grunt, then started spouting profanity. "You'll all regret this, I can promise you that. You have no reason to hold us, you got that? No reason, no proof, no search warrants, nothing. You've got nothing on us, you hear me? You're breaking the law. My lawyer will see you in court."

"I love visiting people in the courtroom," Josie countered as she searched the room, her breath rasping. "I've got enough for now to at least take you both in for questioning. We found some interesting items in your daddy's safe."

Lou's gaze collided with his mother's. "What are they talking about?"

"I . . . I don't know," Vanessa said. "I never got past the garage. Someone threw something through a window and . . . the fire started and spread across the floor." She looked genuinely frightened. "Lou, we've got to stop this."

"Shut up!" her son shouted. His frowning face pulsed with an angry twitch. "I'm telling you, Randall, you will regret this."

Connor took the sturdy garbage-bag tie Josie had hurriedly found in the big pantry and tied Lou's hands. Then she did the same for his mother.

"The only thing I regret is that you had your nasty hands on Agent Gilbert," he grated in Lou's ear. "You're done here, Little Lou."

Lou kept cursing and hissing right along with his spitfire mother. By the time the backup agents arrived, they were both tied to dining chairs, and Beaux and Connor held the guns on them while Josie gave a report to Sherwood and the other agents.

"Two more Armonds carted off to the big house," Beaux said on a satisfied sigh after Sherwood had gone back to the garage. "I'm sorry about that, Connor."

"It's okay," Connor retorted, his gaze on Josie.

He breathed a sigh of relief. "I'm so ready to be done with this."

"Me, too," she replied. "But right now, we need to see what the team found in that garage and possibly search it again before it gets trampled and rearranged."

Beaux reluctantly left with the FBI after being promised he'd be under twenty-four-hour protective guard until he could testify against the Armonds. He understood he might have to go into some sort of witness-protection program, but the big man seemed relieved even after hearing that.

Lou shouted at him and called him a dead man walking, but Beaux didn't look back. In separate cars, they were all carted back to the city.

Connor should have been relieved, but he knew this wasn't over yet. It wouldn't be over until they rounded up everyone involved with the Armond dynasty. But that list was long, and it stretched out over the entire world. He didn't have enough time to bring them all in.

But he'd do it just to avoid seeing Josie held at gunpoint ever again.

Hours later in the predawn light, the charred remains of the big garage loomed like a dark hulk over what was left of the rainy night. Josie and Connor moved through the smoldering embers, careful of where they stepped. The forensic team had done a thorough job of bagging and tagging but Josie's gut told her something could still be hidden here.

They'd searched the whole house but had found nothing—no other computers or flash drives, no safes or obvious hiding places. Josie had checked behind paintings and gone through office cabinets. Armond had covered his tracks, except for the contents of that safe. Which stuck out like a sore thumb.

Josie held her flashlight high to shine over their path, lifting crime-scene tape away from the gutted remains. "The forensic team and the parish fire investigator have gone over this entire place, but they didn't find anything out of the ordinary."

"Except the accelerant that they told us about," Connor said. "Someone threw a Molotov cocktail through that side window."

Josie lifted the flashlight to the broken window, then swept it over the fire trail scorched across the floor. She had a vague memory of a hulking shape on the stairs, but it could have just been a shadow. "So an arsonist is now on the loose. I wonder if that person is the same one trying to kill all of us, the same one who set up that low-explosive bomb. Or did someone just want to destroy incriminating materials in both cases?"

"And I wonder why you insisted on staying behind to search again," Connor retorted. "I'm dirty, tired and in need of nourishment. But you, Agent Gilbert, you just keep on ticking."

"I'm exhausted, too," she said on a long sigh. "But both Vanessa and Lou Armond returned here for something. That woman was willing to die in this fire to find whatever she believes is in this garage. What if someone was trying to get that money and those invoices *out* of the safe and just ran out of time?"

Connor shrugged. "It's possible. But a team of agents and experts just left without finding a thing," Connor reminded her. "They found the source of the fire but nothing to pin on anyone."

"But they'll definitely question the Armonds— you can count on that. For all we know, Vanessa started the fire. I did find her near the side door." She glanced up at the stairs again.

"I understand she's a suspect, and I'm extremely glad she and Little Lou are in good hands now," he said, "but don't you think we should get out of here before somebody else shows up?"

She whirled on him. "Stop trying to convince me to leave, and start thinking like a criminal, okay? You do remember how to do that, don't you?"

Surprised, he tugged a hand through his hair. "You want me to think like a criminal?"

"Yes." She held the flashlight down. "There is something very valuable in here, something that could either make someone rich or do someone a lot of harm. Could it have been in one of those upper rooms?"

Connor stared up what was left of the stairs. "He did store things up there. He's a collector, so who knows what he's stashed and where."

"We need to pin something down," Josie replied.

Connor ticked off the obvious. "They came after Armond by killing Lewanna first. Remember, they sent Lewanna a letter."

Josie pointed the flashlight's beam up high. "Yes. We turned that over to Sherwood already, but nothing to go on there yet. So Armond overstepped his boundaries or, at the very least, made someone very angry."

"Yes, then they tried to kill Armond again at the hotel, which was supposed to be a safe house."

"True. And then they came after us at Mama Joe's. But why? Do they think you have what they're looking for?"

"Or maybe they want both of us out of the way," Connor replied. "If Lou had wanted us dead, he would have killed us tonight. I think he needed us alive. He did try to take you with him."

"That man's too caught up in being an Armond to let anyone live," Josie said. "I took him down with an elbow and a swift kick, but I still believe he could be very dangerous."

"Yeah, he's led the good life for so long he's definitely out of shape. And apparently out of the loop. Not knowing can certainly make a man do crazy things."

"Do you think he's the silent partner no one knows about? Maybe his daddy did something Lou didn't approve of, based on that cryptic note Lewanna received."

Connor shook his head. "Armond wouldn't make Lou his partner. I'm thinking this partner is feeling the heat, so he wants Armond out of the picture. He's probably been playing Armond, stringing him along until the perfect opportunity presents itself."

Josie lifted the flashlight again. "Keep your enemies close and pretend to not know anything?"

"Possibly. Maybe the partner knows Armond has another son somewhere out there and he's planning to use that information."

She shrugged and flicked the light again. "Back to you thinking like a criminal. If you were a bad guy—which you are not now, thankfully—where would you hide something important? I mean something maybe with historical or artistic value? Or possibly an incriminating value. Or maybe even both."

Connor didn't understand where she was coming from at first, but then it hit him. "Or what if you were trying to hide something very secretive and extremely damaging *inside* an artifact or piece of art?"

"Now, that's thinking like a criminal," Josie said, all smiles. "And that's smart."

"We need to find a way upstairs," he replied.

She moved a step forward at the same time Connor did, and they collided in the only open path left in the charred and melted garage.

Connor caught her against him, his eyes meeting hers as she stumbled into his arms. "Sorry," he mumbled, his lips so close to hers he could see the sweet pink of her lip gloss in the growing morning light.

"That's okay." She tried to move but somehow wound up tripping over a fallen beam.

Connor caught her again, and this time he didn't let her go. "Josie . . ."

She gave a little moan and then their lips were together, exploring and experimenting. Around them, the smell of burned wood and melted metal permeated the air. But here, with her in his arms, Connor smelled what was left of the clean scent of her hair and the faint hint of her spicy shower gel and shampoo.

After a minute or two, he lifted his head and held his forehead to hers. "Why is it, Agent Gilbert, that being in tight spots with you seems to bring out all my romantic notions?"

Josie's eyes burned an amber-gold. "I . . . I don't know. I can't explain it. Maybe the danger. Is that intoxicating for you?"

"No, but you are," he said, his hand moving down her soft, sooty cheek. "You do things to me, Josie. When that idiot Lou had that gun to your head, I . . . I couldn't breathe. I wanted to hurt him in slow, torturous ways."

"Guns are scary that way."

"But you were as cool as a Popsicle."

"A Popsicle? Seriously?"

"Icy and bright and . . . I don't know. I don't know how to describe it."

She held her free hand on his shoulder. "I was anything but cool, trust me. But I had to think of how to get us all out of there alive."

"Do you think Lou would have killed us?"

"In a heartbeat."

"I lost a few heartbeats when he had his hands on you."

"And here I thought you were the cool customer."

"I used to be," he admitted. "But that was before I had a change of heart. And that was before I met you."

"I need you to stay cool, Connor," she said. "I need you to keep thinking with that ruthlessness you've always had. If you go soft on me now, we could both wind up dead."

"I'm not going soft," he replied, his heart beating with a new strength. "Except when I kiss you."

He kissed her again. But a ping of a shoe hitting concrete in the back of the garage brought them apart. Taking Josie by the hand, he pulled her behind a collapsed wall.

"I don't think we're alone anymore."

Josie nodded, then looked around for an escape. "Here we go again. Will this night ever be over?"

THIRTEEN. . .

"Shh."

Connor put a finger to his lips.

Josie drew her gun, but held her breath. Who could be snooping around now? The FBI and the ATF had posted guards all over the property and the sheriff's department had patrol cars roaming the roads and woods. Everyone wanted a piece of the Armond case, so all of the local agencies were cooperating on this one.

Connor lifted his head a notch so he could see between two burned-out, wet beams. He held up one finger.

Josie tried to speak. "One man?"

"Yes." He squinted again, then turned to her. "It's Sherwood."

"My SAC?"

Connor's right eyebrow twitched. "Can we trust him, Josie?"

"Of course." But even as she said it, she had to wonder. No, that was crazy. Sherwood was a staunch family man who'd dedicated his life to the FBI, and he'd been trying to pin something on Louis Armond long before she arrived on the scene. The man had spent most of his career trying to bring down the Mafia lord.

"We need to alert him that we're here," she whispered.

"Are you sure?"

That little trickle of doubt dripped down her spine. "We can't hide from the man. We're checking the scene of the fire."

Connor's brow furrowed. "Whatever you say, but I'll be watching him. In my mind, everyone is a suspect."

"Yeah, well, in the eyes of the law, we're all innocent until proven guilty."

"Who's there?"

Josie heard Sherwood's gruff call. Too late to change her mind now. "It's me, sir. Gilbert. Connor Randall is with me."

"Come on out where I can see you."

Josie motioned to Connor, then proceeded with her gun down. When she came around the collapsed wall, Sherwood was standing with his gun drawn.

"Sir?"

He lowered the gun and let out a breath of relief. "Thought I was a goner for a minute there." Keeping his weapon aimed down, he stepped over old tires and an overturned toolbox. "You two still hanging around?"

"We wanted to do one more search," Josie explained. "Vanessa Armond was definitely looking for something in here."

Sherwood took off his FBI ball cap and scratched his head. "Gilbert, you never give up, do you? We had a team of experts from three different law-enforcement offices in here, and they only found what you see—a burned-up building with a lot of automotive junk in it." He pointed toward the big window. "Someone threw the accelerant through that window, so we know it was arson. I'm liking Vanessa Armond for it. She had means and she had motive. She's a woman scorned, and now word is out that her husband's mistress was murdered. She came back for revenge and made it look like she was trapped when she saw you."

"Maybe what Vanessa was looking for is in one of the vehicles you confiscated," Connor suggested, his gaze cutting toward Sherwood. For someone who'd been shot, his mobility in both arms was remarkable.

"Thanks for that expert assumption, Randall," Sherwood drawled. "But you two have gone off on one too many wild-goose chases over the past few days. I think we need to regroup and get back on track. Your reports still have a few holes to fill."

"What is our track?" Josie asked, wondering why he had come back to the garage. "Did you find out anything else that we need to know?"

"Nope, not a thing. I just wanted to have one more look myself. Too many people hanging around this place. Like you, I figured something important must be hidden here."

"All kinds of places to hide things," Connor said, walking around, his head up. "Those stairs had to lead to somewhere."

"Not anymore," Sherwood said. "Interesting that the fire was set very near that upstairs apartment."

"The hired help did stay out here," Josie said, giving Connor a quick glance. She should have gone up there first thing, but the whole place was a safety hazard.

"But why would the hired help hide something important to the Armonds?" Connor kept his eyes on Sherwood.

"Employees have been known to go off the grid, Randall," the older man said, his gray eyes turning crystal. "You should know all about that."

"I've been paying my dues to the FBI," Connor retorted. "I only went off the grid this time to find out who's trying to kill Armond. I've been undercover with the man for a while now. Or at least I was until that night of the Benoit heist."

"A failed heist," Sherwood reminded him. "But hey, you did find three canvases worth millions of dollars." Then he asked, "Do you have any suspects you'd like to share?"

Josie watched as this showdown became more aggressive. Getting between the two men, she put up a hand. "We know Armond is a criminal, but we have to have proof of that, and so far, we don't have anything on him except possibly the murder of his mistress and the cash and invoices. But his wife and son are hiding something, and they did hold us at gunpoint. We need to find out what that something is."

"We're all in danger," Connor said. "We can't stop now. And you can't hold the Armonds for long."

"Louis is still in and out of consciousness," Sherwood said. He tramped around debris so he could move closer but Josie noticed his gaze darting here and there. "The wife and son have lawyered up enough that they'll probably get away with a slap on the hand for holding y'all. Beaux Perot, however, has been a wealth of information. He might become our strongest witness."

"That's good," Josie replied. "I'd love a go at him. Beaux seems like a good man caught in a bad situation."

"Good men have been known to go bad," Sherwood said, his hostile gaze settling on Connor. "I think we need to get back to town. Need a lift?"

"No, we have a car," Connor said before Josie could respond.

Okay. Why did he say that? Beaux had brought

them out in his SUV. It had gone back to the city for a thorough inspection.

"We'll be along shortly, sir," she said. "Mind if we have one last look around?"

"Not at all," Sherwood said, his expression edged with distaste. "Just don't do anything stupid, Gilbert. You're still a probbie in my mind."

"Yes, sir." She watched him go, then when he was out of sight, she turned to Connor. "What was that all about?"

"We need to do one more search," Connor said on a low breath. "I've learned to read people and, Josie, I'm telling you, something is off with your boss."

"You're imagining things," she retorted on a curt whisper. "And I'm in enough trouble. Let's look around, then get out of here." She whirled. "Oh, wait. We don't have a car, do we?"

"Actually, I know where Armond keeps another garage," Connor said. "And I know a car that will get us back to town in a hurry."

"You've been holding out on me," she said as they retraced their steps and peered into the daylight filtering through the gaping hole in the roof. And she had to wonder, what else was he hiding?

"No, I think I mentioned it in passing. He has lots of outbuildings around here. But this is a small wooden shed, not what I'd call a garage."

"Right." Josie lifted tools and shuffled through old rags before opening toolboxes and hardware drawers. Nothing stood out. But this place was like a giant cave, and the upstairs rooms were completely cut off and burned out.

Then they both turned to each other. "Another garage."

"Armond has another garage," Connor said, his eyes wide.

"And maybe, just maybe, that's where he's hiding the something we're all looking for. Lead the way, please."

Josie made a production of bowing and holding her arm out. But she had to wonder why Connor had just now remembered such a vital piece of information.

"Great, more swamp."

Josie's boots slushed through the dark, rich loam as she batted away both bugs and palmetto leaves. "I'm beginning to hate Louisiana."

"More than Texas?"

She ignored that baited question. "I loved Texas. I mean, I grew up there."

"Now we're getting somewhere," Connor replied. He stomped ahead of her, using a big stick he'd found from a fallen branch to hit at possible poisonous snakes. "So you're a Texas native."

"Born and bred." She stopped to take a breath

and to carefully measure her answers. "My father moved among the upper crust of Houston. He also took a lot of their money." She shrugged and pushed at her damp hair. "I think that's why my mother left Texas. She couldn't take the pain of her friends abandoning her."

Nor the pain of her daughter's judgment and scorn, Josie thought.

Connor knocked down a twisted vine. "Do you ever visit your father in prison?"

"I haven't in a while. We don't have much to talk about."

She thought about Dallas and the undercover operation that had gone bad. She couldn't afford to mess up this time. She'd wind up old and alone like her mother.

"There it is," Connor said, turning to help her the last few feet.

"That's a garage?"

The old lean-to looked as if it might fall over if they touched it. "There's a car in there?"

"Armond is a man of many surprises." Connor moved through the bramble toward the building. "He liked to hide things in odd places, which is probably why we can't find anything interesting around the house or the big garage."

"And you just happen to know about this car?"

"He showed it to me once when he was in a melancholy mood. This was his first car."

Josie glanced around to make sure they didn't

get picked up by a sheriff's deputy. "Why haven't you mentioned this earlier?"

Connor cut his gaze to her. "Are you curious or are you interrogating me for a reason?"

"It's just odd that we've spent most of the night trying to find something in the big fancy garage when you knew about this one all along."

Connor stopped to give her a harsh stare. "Hey, we've been kind of busy for the past few days and we only realized something might be hidden in the garage after Beaux mentioned it and then you saved Vanessa Armond, remember? So we focused on that garage. Or do you still not trust me? Josie?"

Josie let out a sigh and then grunted out her frustration. "Okay, all right. We'll talk about all of it on the way into town after we've searched every inch of this place. Let's hope we find something to give us a clue and let's hope this vehicle will crank."

Connor opened the rickety old door and set it back against some shrub oaks. Inside the dark interior, Josie heard a scuffling.

"Rats or nutria," Connor warned. "Nasty creatures."

"Thanks for telling me that," she replied with a grimace. "What else could be in here?"

He tapped the dirt floors with the rickety limb. "Snakes, of course. Spiders."

The vehicle was covered in a heavy gray

canvas. Connor tossed her the stick and then pulled the cover off the car.

She let out a gasp this time. "A '63 Camaro."

"A Z-28, at that."

"Can you drive this thing?"

"Of course I can. Armond let me take it for a spin back when we got so buddy-buddy."

"Let's search it first."

While they checked over the car, she wondered just how buddy-buddy he and Armond had gotten. Armond had called on Connor to help him out of a big jam, but that had been more like a summons—as in flesh owed him. She really wanted to figure out the dynamics of that relationship. It sure seemed mighty convenient that Connor had been on the scene just in time to help Armond. Coincidence or part of the plan? This case didn't make a bit of sense, and her gut kept reminding her that Connor was still caught between two worlds. Which route would he really take when push came to shove?

After a half hour or so, Connor came around to the driver's side. "Nothing. This car is clean as a whistle, if you ignore the pollen and dust."

Josie leaned in one more time. "Just an old necklace."

Connor looked at the gold coin dangling on an old chain over the rearview mirror. "Yeah. I don't remember that being there, but Armond has a thing for gold."

"I noticed that in his furnishings."

"Let's go." He got in and waited for her. "I'll check out the coin later."

Josie slid into the low black leather seat. "Does it have gas?"

"We'll see."

Connor did a little hot-wiring and cranked the car. The engine purred like a contented tiger. "Plenty of fuel. He kept it full and usually he'd sneak out about once a week and give it a spin around the country roads. Said this was his guilty pleasure. We laughed a lot that day." He shrugged. "Armond's son hates him. I guess I made up for that."

"You really like the old man, don't you?"

"I do," he admitted. Looking over his shoulder, he backed out of the old garage. "But not enough to become his made man. Once, I would have jumped at the chance, but that changed when I realized my sister was afraid of me."

"What made her so afraid?"

He kept his gaze on the dirt lane. "She works for Princess Lara Kincade, and last year things kind of came to a head when Deidre saw me back in New Orleans. She was afraid I'd followed them from Europe to steal the Benoits. She almost quit her job, she was so afraid."

He stopped at the road out and turned to gaze at Josie, his eyes burning with remorse. "I'll never forget the look on my sister's face when she confronted me. It was the same look she had when we were little and I had to leave her behind."

Well, that was certainly a new revelation. Something inside Josie's heart melted away, leaving her standing in quicksand. "You love your sister more than you love Armond and a life of crime?"

"Yes. Deidre's taught me about faith and love —unconditional love." He shook his head. "Look, we don't have time for a devotional but just know this, Josie. You can trust me. You have to trust me."

"I do. I will," she said, still not sure. And because she couldn't deal with his raw honesty right now, she added, "Can I trust you to get me back to New Orleans without getting a speeding ticket?"

"Absolutely," he said on a grin. "I know all the back roads."

"A muscle car," she said, shaking her head. "Criminals can be so eclectic about things."

"Armond fits that mold," Connor said, his hand on the gearshift. "One minute, I'd think I had him, and the next he'd be in such a foul mood no one, including me, wanted to be around him. He always seemed secretive, but at times he sounded downright depressed."

"A life of lies and crime can do that to a man."

"I should know that." He glanced over at her. "One day, I want to be able to walk down a street without having to look behind me."

Josie's heart did another little shift. That made her mad. She didn't want to like this man and she sure didn't want to be attracted to him. But when he kissed her . . . her whole world became blurred and confused. She'd stepped over a mighty big line, and now she couldn't go back.

Did she want to go back?

She glanced over at Connor. He was dirty, windblown and gritty right now, but he still did things to her.

"What?" he asked, giving her that slanted look that always took hold of her heart.

Josie shook her head. "I don't know. Still trying to figure you out."

"You need to give up on that."

"Why? Afraid I'll get too close?"

"You are too close."

So he felt the same way. Or had he purposely tried to confuse her?

"We have to stay on track," she said. "We're running out of Armonds."

"I won't stop until they're all either turned or in jail."

"But you said you didn't have much on them. Have you been holding out on the FBI?"

"No. I've shared things with the FBI to build a file and a case, but it was never enough to bring him in. For two long years I've worked hard to gain Armond's trust. I expected the man to kill me several times over. The puzzle is this—why hasn't he? And why did he turn to me the other night?"

"He thought he had you cornered," Josie said. "By the way, why did you agree to meet him at the opera? We went along with it, but now that I look back that seems crazy, considering we wanted to bring him in without any fanfare."

He winked at her. "It was *La Bohème.*"

"I get that you're into Italian operas, but you had another reason for being there. Or maybe he did."

He finally nodded. "I wanted to spy on Armond *before* I met with him. I thought if I got something else on him, I could use it against him as leverage when we had our little talk."

"A gift to the FBI or payback with Armond?"

"I'm not above blackmailing a criminal to get out of a jam."

"Why at the opera?"

"He conducts a lot of business in his balcony box."

"So you dressed up and planned to what . . . stand in the corner and listen in, or maybe sit down beside him and ask him to tell you something you could use against him?"

"It wasn't like that. I wanted to see who would be meeting him there."

"Oh, and how did you know he'd be meeting someone else there?"

He hesitated, then glanced over at her. "You

won't like this, but I *haven't* told you everything."

Josie's heart pulled back up to solid ground. Of course he hadn't told her everything. Hadn't she felt this coming? "You just told me you had. Talk, Connor, and this time, don't leave anything out."

Connor's expression filled with regret and resolve. "Sometimes, he'd dismiss all his guards and go alone to his box seats. And I mean alone. I never was invited to attend with him, but I've gone to the opera house several times to see if I could figure out who he was meeting." He maneuvered the car around a sharp curve. "I thought maybe it was Lewanna. His guards weren't around when she got shot."

"But you obviously didn't see anyone else."

"No. I was getting close—I'd dismissed several people as bit players. I'm beginning to wonder if maybe his son wasn't showing up. *His other son,* that is. Whoever it was always slipped away before anyone knew."

"Did you know there might be another son?"

Connor shifted gears and turned onto another stretch of highway. "I suspected. I was trying to find out who that might be back when the Benoit issue came to a close. But I'm beginning to think no one will ever know for sure."

FOURTEEN . . .

The Camaro lived up to its name.

They'd made it back to the city in record time.

But Josie couldn't enjoy the ride. She stared over at Connor, all the trust built between them crumbling like decayed bricks. "You suspected and yet you failed to mention that because . . . ?"

"Because it's just a hunch, and because I was waiting to see what transpired."

"Waiting? Connor, this isn't about waiting. This is about being honest with me. You didn't speak up when Beaux told us there might be a second son. Are you trying to break free from this man's grip or are you protecting him because you're really on his side?" She turned in the seat and hit a hand on the dash. "You're still playing games with me."

"No," he said, shaking his head. "I should have told you right up front, but I don't have any proof. He just mentioned it once, when we were cruising in this car."

Still reeling, Josie asked, "And what exactly did he say?"

"He told me he wished things could have been different . . . for his sons."

"Sons? Plural."

"I just thought he'd used the wrong term. He looked broken and sad and . . . I don't know . . . my instincts told me he wanted to say more."

"Did you question him?"

"I tried. I asked him about Lou and why he never came around. He gave me a sad smile. He said, 'I don't make him feel loved.' "

"What else did he say, Connor?"

Connor downshifted as they exited the interstate. "He said he wasn't sure who would inherit his estate."

"And?"

"And he replied that another man would get the bulk of it. That's when I figured he had a silent partner."

Josie's mind went into overdrive right along with the zooming car. "A silent partner who is his secret son?"

"I don't know. When I asked him about it, he brushed it aside and changed the subject, but something about that day stayed with me."

"And yet, you didn't tell me any of this until now. How do you expect me to believe anything you say to me?"

"Look, I'm working hard to prove myself, but . . . I told you this is just a hunch. When Beaux told us Armond might have another son, I figured that was why he was so morose and depressed that day."

"You can say that again," she replied, anger shimmering underneath her still-shaky heart. "Nothing about this makes any sense. If I didn't know better, I'd think you've been taking me on a merry chase down a rabbit hole."

"I'm not doing that," he replied. "I want to find out the truth, too. We need to come up with a con to get them all talking."

"No, no cons, no more lies. Just take me to my office."

"I'm taking you to my apartment," Connor said as they cruised through early-morning traffic. "We can shower, eat and get some rest there. And maybe we can do some more research, come up with a plan."

"I don't want to go to your place. I need to report back to the office."

"You can't do that. It's not safe."

She pinned him with a burning glance. "Says who?"

"Me. What if someone is watching your apartment? What if someone in your office is in on this?"

"I've got people handling that."

He gave Josie a quick glance. "You think you've got people handling that."

"So while you've had me on the run, you've also been working behind my back." Putting her hands to her head, she clutched at her hair. "You are seriously driving me nuts, Connor. I can't trust you, and I'm sorry I ever thought I could. Now, take me to my apartment."

Connor decided to oblige her. She was the one who couldn't see what was clearly in front of her. This wasn't just about Armond and him. Somebody wanted her dead, too. If she hadn't managed to duck and crawl away when the shooting had started at Mama Joe's, she would be dead right now. Then the fire and Vanessa Armond luring her inside that burning building. He couldn't figure that one out, since Vanessa could have died, too, but Connor's gut told him Vanessa was planted there to distract Josie.

"Look," he said, hoping she'd be reasonable. "I've learned how to observe people. Vanessa and Lou showing up last night wasn't just a coincidence. I think they set that fire because they wanted to either destroy something permanently . . . or kill both of us. The whole thing smelled of a setup, just like Lewanna showing up at the opera. Just like that paperwork and cash fund in the safe. We're getting too close to the truth, Josie. The heat is on."

She shrugged. "I guess you're good at keeping one foot in the fire, no pun intended."

"I have to keep one foot in the fire to do what the FBI expects of me. And right now, that means I'm sticking by you."

"I can take care of myself," she retorted, her arms across her midsection.

"I believe that. I've seen that. But, Josie, I'm not playing. We have to be careful."

"What about this car? It's a bit conspicuous. You knew exactly where to find it and now you have it. What if you know what everyone is looking for and you've found it?"

Weariness zapped at Connor's bones. "Are you serious?"

"Deadly serious," she replied, her body shifting as close to the passenger-side door as possible.

"We had to get back to town," he explained. "And if I'd wanted to take this car, I could have done it long ago. I could be somewhere on a beach right now, but I'm not. I'm here with you because I want to be here. You need to remember that."

"What I need to remember is that you were once a criminal. And you know what they say—"

"Stop it," he replied. He didn't have to prove himself to her or anyone else. "Let's just get somewhere safe."

"Right now, I think that would be away from you."

"You need to trust me," Connor said. What more did she want? No matter how much she might doubt him, he intended to keep Josie safe.

At the next traffic stop, he pulled out his phone

and hit the keys. When the light changed, he dropped the phone back into his pocket. "I never text and drive," he explained. "But the word is out and we will be watched and protected while we're in the city. Even criminals have a network, and sometimes I have to depend on it."

"Amazing." Josie sat with her head slanted, staring over at him. "You steal vintage cars and associate with criminals, but you have a code of ethics regarding cell phones and honor among thieves?"

"I do have my standards," he replied on a curt tone.

She gave him another Josie glare. "I'm not so sure I should be alone with you on your own turf. Dangerous. You're still holding out on me."

"That's the last of my secrets," he said. Connor didn't know how to make her believe in him. He'd never come this far with a woman before. He'd never thought it possible.

With Josie, it might not be possible. And why was it the one thing he now wanted most seemed so far out of his reach?

But how could he blame her?

She'd been conned all of her life by a father who pretended to be someone he wasn't. How could Connor expect her to ever see who he truly was, the man he wanted to become?

You just keep doing what you need to do.

And what if that wasn't enough?

He pulled the car up to her Garden District apartment. "I'm going in with you."

She got out before he'd put the car in Park. "You don't need to do that." Josie took off up the gravel lane toward the two-story house. "Just remember to report to either me or Sherwood. I've got my own reports, and I'm sure I'll hear a good chewing-out from my boss."

Connor got out of the car. "Josie, wait. Please?"

She kept walking.

He followed.

She'd made it up the porch to the first door on the left, her keys in her hand. But when she got there, she touched the door and immediately drew her weapon.

The door was open.

Connor rushed up behind her. "I told you it wasn't safe."

"Shh." She entered carefully, her gun trained on the hallway.

Connor stayed right behind her, his gaze taking in the broken locks on the door and the scattered books and papers lining the long hall.

When Josie turned to the left, she stopped and glanced back at him. "I guess you were right, after all."

He didn't want to be right. "I'm sorry," he said. He started past her.

"Wait!" She hurried around him, her gun up

while she checked the bathroom, bedroom and kitchen.

The whole place was ruined. Shattered dishes, broken lamps and knickknacks, clothes tossed, pillows gutted and spewing foam and feathers.

Josie stood at the end of the hall and stared. Thinking she was in shock, Connor tried to reach out to her. "Josie?"

She turned on him, her eyes a burning golden-green. "I'm fine. You don't have to handle me with kid gloves. I won't break, Connor. I never break."

"I know," he said, his heart doing enough breaking for both of them. "But you're coming home with me."

"No." She went into action. "Don't touch anything. I have to call this in, and we have to preserve the scene. I'm sure they didn't leave any prints, but we can dust the door and . . . anything they might have touched." She looked around. "Which seems to be everything."

Connor watched as she walked over to a broken picture of a smiling little girl with two adults. Her parents? She stared down at the image, then moved her fingers over the shattered glass. With a gasp, she put it down and stared at her hand.

Blood poured from her wound.

"Here, let me help you," Connor said, taking her hand in his.

"No. I told you I'm fine. Now get out of the way and let me do my job."

He ignored that and went to the kitchen, found a paper towel and wet it. Then he came back and took her hand again. "You're bleeding. You'll be the one to contaminate the scene."

She stared across at him, her eyes still blazing, her hair wild and tumbled around her face. "I don't need you," she said, her anger boiling over. "Do you understand me, Connor? I don't need you."

"I know." He kept touching the cool paper towel to her cut. "I know."

She yanked away and dialed 911, then called Sherwood.

Then she started taking pictures of each room, her phone clicking as she went. After each picture, she jotted notes on her notebook app, her thoroughness as solid as her dislike of him.

But Connor wasn't finished with her. Not by a long shot.

Because he'd seen something else there in her fiery gaze.

Hurt.

She'd been hurt, and now she was trying very hard to hide that hurt behind an FBI shield.

He wanted to be the man to take that hurt away. But before he could do that, he needed to prove to her that he could be worthy of the task.

FIFTEEN . . .

"My apartment is off the beaten path and I have good security. The FBI knows where I live, but they tend to stay away from here. The only reason I haven't been back here is because we've been forced to stay on the move since I first called you. Time for a break from the bad guys."

Connor had tried every tactic to get Josie to talk, but she wasn't in the mood for conversation. She kept jotting notes on her phone notepad. And ignoring him.

He'd had to do some tall talking back at her place to get Sherwood to let her come with him.

The SAC had a whole team moving through Josie's ransacked apartment. "She's my agent, Randall. And all this running around on your own ends right now. You're chasing shadows and that's all you know. Agent Gilbert knows how to do her job with or without you."

Connor had never liked Sherwood, but he ignored that dig and concentrated on persuading the man. "Look, sir, with all due respect, we did manage to hand over three members of the Armond family to you. If you give us another chance, I think we can figure this out."

"We're running out of chances," Sherwood

retorted. "I've let you get away with a lot, Randall. It's time to finish this."

"You have Armond," Connor replied. "Maybe if Josie and I talk to him—"

"He's not talking," Sherwood retorted, his face lined with a gray weariness. "He's still not out of the woods. He got through surgery but he's an old man. He can't have a lot of visitors. Besides, I've questioned him, and he's not giving us anything that we don't already know."

Connor didn't believe that. "I could persuade him—"

"I said no. Stay away from Armond. You'll bring the killers right to his hospital room."

Connor finally gave up on that, but he wouldn't give up on protecting Josie. "Josie needs to stay hidden, too. With me."

Sherwood's scowl shouted *NO*. "Gilbert needs to get back to the office first thing next week and you need to remember I'm watching you."

"And what about Josie, sir? Who's watching out for her?"

Sherwood hadn't liked that question. "Maybe I should separate you two so she can get on with her job."

"Not tonight, not after the past few days," Connor had replied. "She's not staying here in this apartment and she's sure not staying alone any-where in this city. She'll be with me for the weekend at least."

"If anything happens to her, it's on you," Sherwood had retorted.

It's on me.

Sometimes, Connor felt as if it was all on him.

He glanced back over at Josie. She was mad and frustrated and she'd put up a good fight, but she had gotten in the car with him. That was a good sign.

"I'm not worried about the bad guys," she finally said. Shutting off her phone, she pushed at her hair and gave him a daring stare. "Right now, I'm only worried about one questionably good guy who forced me into this car."

"*Moi?*"

"*Oui,*" she replied, the one word more confident than the confusion in her eyes. "I agreed to come with you because I'm tired, Connor. Tired and determined to keep eyes on you."

He said the words slowly. "You are safe with me. You can trust me. We've got two days. You can get some rest and rethink this whole thing."

"Famous last words."

He skirted Canal and took side streets in a zigzag pattern. "I don't think anyone is following us, but just in case."

They'd found nothing to help them at her house. Just a destroyed apartment, which only proved someone was looking for something. A file or a thumb drive? A notebook or a stack of letters and receipts? What? What could it be?

And who?

Connor used to be the hunter, the one watching for routines and patterns and changes. Now he and Josie were being hunted. And for what? And where was Armond?

Josie stayed alert the whole trip, watching in the passenger-side mirror when she wasn't eyeballing him through a grumpy glare.

"My clothes are ruined again," she said, staring down at the jacket and slacks she'd been wearing all night and most of the day.

"I have clothes."

"Of course you do."

"Deidre left some things in my apartment last time she was stateside."

"Just to test your *no more secrets* theory, tell me about Deidre?"

Connor smiled at that, but he didn't mind the interrogation. Josie never just asked a question. She was still looking for answers. "My sister is cute but bookish, smart but shy, lovable but reserved. She could be a real beauty if she'd let anyone near enough to get her new glasses and a new wardrobe. I love her, but she hasn't always loved me."

"But she's your half sister, right?"

He nodded, memories of growing up with his sweet little sister always centered in his mind. "And like me, she never knew who her father was." He shrugged. "Our mother was unconventional at best. She never needed a man except for the occasional companion. She didn't believe in God or Jesus. She only believed in herself. Thought she could conquer the world." He downshifted when they reached a crumbling parking garage. "But in the end, the world conquered her."

"I'm sorry," Josie said, "about you and Deidre not having fathers, about how your mother died. I can see why you became so desperate after you realized she was bankrupt."

"I was never desperate," he corrected, his rage always simmering just below the truth. Her curt question brought it all back. She couldn't trick him into any kind of confession, though. "But I was hungry and afraid, and I wanted to feed my sister. We lost everything after our mother was killed."

He pulled the purring car up onto a ramp, then rolled down the window to hit a button. The ramp lifted them up four floors with an elevator-like precision and stopped in front of another elevator.

Killing the engine, he turned to Josie. "They wanted to take Deidre away, since she was underage. I had just turned eighteen, but she was only fourteen. I took her with me and I made sure she was with people I could trust before I left her. I came to America because I had ties here in New Orleans, through my mother. I camped out in this building and did what I had to do to survive. I'm not proud of some of the things I did, but as long as Deidre . . . and God . . . have forgiven me, I can live with that."

"Maybe you should forgive yourself," Josie said, her tone quiet and accepting now.

Connor didn't want to talk about forgiveness. "I've been working on that one for years."

He opened the car door to get out, then noticed the gold coin dangling on a chain around the rearview mirror. In all the fuss, he'd forgotten about it. Grabbing it, Connor decided he would indulge in studying the necklace later.

"I've always had a thing for old coins," he explained when Josie gave him a questioning look.

"You stole the car. Might as well take the coin, too."

"I didn't steal the car. I borrowed it. Armond will understand."

"Really? The man who wants you dead but can't make up his mind to whack you? That man will understand?"

"He has a heart underneath all that . . . illegal stuff," Connor admitted. "At least, I think so."

"Right."

She obviously still didn't believe anything he or Armond had to say.

Connor put the long chain around his neck and tucked it inside his shirt. He came around the car and was about to open her door, but Josie beat him to that and got out to glance around. "This place is a dump."

"That's right. My dump."

He guided her toward the old industrial elevator. "Your next ride is waiting, m'lady."

Josie wondered what to expect, but then Connor had taken her to some strange places over the past few days. She couldn't blame him for some-one deciding to tear apart the home she'd set up just a few weeks ago. She traveled light and that stuff could be replaced.

Connor's holding back on her tore at her and worried her. Sherwood thought they'd been taken down a merry road to nowhere and maybe they had. But she'd brought him Armond and family. And she was bone tired with this whole case. She wouldn't rest until she'd cracked the whole thing.

She needed to talk to Louis Armond. She didn't trust anyone else to tell her what he could.

And she wouldn't let Sherwood or Connor hold her back on that decision. She'd have to find the right time, then she'd have to find the right hospital. But she would find Armond.

"Hungry?"

She glanced over at Connor as they rode up the rickety old elevator. "No."

Wishing for some of Mama Joe's biscuits, she held on and took a deep breath. "So I love what you've done with the place."

Connor laughed and touched a hand to her frazzled, smoke-scented hair. "You need a bath, Special Agent Gilbert."

"You sure know how to make a girl feel lovely, Randall."

"Part of my speciality."

His eyes promised more, but Josie decided going back to an all-business stance had to be the best plan. "So we need to consider that we might not ever find anything on Armond's silent partner. The house has been wiped clean, either by several different law-enforcement agencies or . . . someone else. The garage is toast and we really didn't get to do a very thorough search."

"I'm thinking after seeing your place your supervisor will send a forensic team back out there to make sure we didn't miss anything. At least now he believes we're both still in danger. Which is why we have to stay away from Armond Gardens."

"You really don't like Sherwood, do you?"

He gave her a blank stare. "No, I don't."

She needed to remember that he probably didn't trust anyone in the FBI, especially her. That worked both ways. But they were in this together now, and Sherwood would expect her to do her job.

Even if that meant betraying the man standing in front of her. The man she was so angry with right now, but to whom she was still so very attracted.

●●●

An hour later Josie emerged from the guest-room bath and threw on the clothes Connor had handed her earlier. He'd picked a soft blue cardigan, a light blue button-up shirt and a pair of worn jeans that held a hint of lavender. The jeans were about an inch too short, so Josie rolled them up to capri length and decided that would do.

When she picked up the expensive shirt, her heart slammed to her feet. She knew this scent. This shirt didn't belong to Deidre. It belonged to her big brother. Putting the cotton garment to her nose, Josie inhaled Connor's aftershave, silly tears pricking her eyes and making her throat grow tight.

She wouldn't let him get to her. Looking down at the cut on her palm, she remembered how gentle he'd been with her earlier.

The little gestures got to her more than any grand gesture ever would. She slipped on the too-big shirt and buttoned it, feeling safe and comfortable surrounded by something of his.

But he's lying to you, Josie. You have to see that. He's lying and he's covering for Armond.

Why?

Why couldn't she believe him?

Closing her eyes to that admission, she tugged on the lightweight sweater and then rolled up the shirt's sleeves.

Then she told herself to stop being so mushy

and get back to business. Connor's new revelation about another possible Armond son was ridiculous, but . . . he had been around Armond more than she had. His instincts were good on such matters, too.

In spite of everything, she wanted to believe him. She wanted to believe in him, too.

After she dressed, she took her time studying Connor's home. Eclectic and sterile. Edited and minimalist. Artsy and comfortable. The old industrial building held a hint of steam-punk mixed with a futuristic vibe.

A lot like Connor. Old-fashioned and gentlemanly, but edgy and hip, too. The man knew his art. Twisted metal sculptures merged with watercolor still-life scenes and spiritual Impressionist paintings. The chunky wooden bed in this room looked antique, but the stark red-and-gold painting of a lone jester who was not smiling showed the paradox of Connor's life.

That painting made her heart bump against her chest in a sympathetic tone that both thrilled her and annoyed her. When she saw an antique Bible on the Rococo-style dresser, she opened it and saw marked pages. Connor? Or maybe Deidre?

Thankfully, his sister's influence had turned him back to the Lord. Josie closed her eyes in prayer for both of them and for herself, her fingers touching on the always-comforting passages of the Psalms.

She didn't want to want this man in her life but after being around him 24/7 for the past few days, Josie knew she'd feel like that sad-faced jester if she lost Connor now. Befriend and betray. Was that what they were doing to each other? That was what her job required.

After drying her hair, Josie slid open the heavy metal bedroom door and walked back out into the open-air loft. Apparently Connor's bedroom was up on the top tier of this interesting place. He'd gone up there to get his own shower and change of clothing.

She pushed at her hair and took in the dark leather couches and worn tapestry patterned armchairs, the shelves of books and the walls of artifacts and paintings. The kitchen beckoned with a gleaming industrial shine, so she headed that way and opened the refrigerator to find boiled shrimp resting on ice.

When had he ordered in?

Josie didn't question this gift. She was starving, so she took out the big bowl and grabbed a couple of the fat, juicy shrimp and dipped them in the thick red cocktail sauce. They tasted fresh and spicy. When she heard him coming down the metal stairs, she turned and smiled and gulped in a breath.

He was barefoot and in jeans and a faded T-shirt.

A different kind of Connor.

"I found food," she said, nervous now that they were alone. Which was silly, since they'd been traveling around alone for days now. "I don't know how this got here, but I'm glad it did."

"I called a friend who works as a chef in one of my favorite restaurants." He pointed to the counter. "We have pecan-crusted trout and a side salad, too."

Josie let out a yelp of joy, then quickly dived into the fish, taking a nibble with a low moan of appreciation. "You do have connections." Then she turned FBI again. "This chef, can we trust him?"

"Yes. He owes me."

She figured a lot of people owed him, and she did not want to ask why. "And dessert?"

"Of course. Caramel crème brûlée."

She had to hold on to the shimmering steel counter. "I could stay with you forever just based on the food."

When she realized what she'd said, Josie looked up at him there across the counter from her, her mouth opening in shock and awareness.

Before she could change her comment to something more reasonable and not so adoring, Connor stalked around the long counter and pulled her into his arms.

The kiss was demanding and sweet, a contradiction, just like the man. He pulled her hair through his hands and pressed his palms against her head. "Josie . . ."

Josie lifted her lips away, her gaze holding his. "We can't do this, Connor. We can't—"

"Says who? Is there some rule in the FBI handbook about this?"

She searched for her next breath. "Lots of rules, and we're breaking all of them."

"I don't care."

"But I do."

She backed up, pushed at her tousled hair. "I do and I'm sorry."

"What if I wasn't me and you weren't FBI?"

"Things might be different then."

He moved away, leaned back against the deep sink. "I've changed, Josie. I'm on the right side of the law now. I pray for forgiveness but I want acceptance." Shoving off the sink counter, he started covering the food. "I long for you to . . . accept me. I've tried to be honest with you. Do you hear me? This is not one of my cons."

Josie wanted to believe that. But they had so much between them. "We have a job to do, Connor. You're all tied up in this case. I'm your handler, the person you have to report back to, the person who's supposed to watch out for you and advise you and protect you. Nothing about this makes any sense because you don't have any information and neither do I."

"You think I'm playing you, right? You think

I'm faking all of this and that I'm still in cahoots with Armond?"

"Yes," she said, wishing she didn't think that way. "I trust you with my life, but I can't trust you to tell me the truth."

He hit a hand on the counter, jarring the crystal goblets sitting on a silver tray. "What do you want me to say?"

"I want you to tell me everything you can remember about being on the inside of Armond's organization. We can't keep running."

She let go of the counter and stared out the big square windows covering one wall. The city twinkled around them and the sound of music echoed out into the night, a lone saxophone playing. Probably Harold down at the Café du Monde. The Mississippi wrapped like a dark velvet blanket through the city on one side, while the St. Louis Cathedral shone in an abiding light off to the left.

This was the kind of night that could mess with a woman's head. The soft, soulful music drifting up into the sparkling stars, the river following the tide, the food, this room, this man. That kiss.

She turned to find Connor staring at her, his eyes a deep, burning blue. "I think you're the one who needs to be honest, Agent Gilbert. I can feel how you feel when you're in my arms, so you can't hide that. But you need to be honest with me and you need to be honest with yourself."

"What could I possibly be hiding?"

"Everything," he said. Then he turned and went back up to the loft.

Josie wanted to call out to him to come back. Instead, she put the tempting shrimp back in the refrigerator. Then she moved closer to the window and wondered who out there wanted both of them dead.

And she also wondered if she'd ever know the real Connor Randall.

SIXTEEN . . .

Her dreams were mixed in swirls of clinging tropical vines and dark raging waters twisted into moments of running for her life through the swamp. She tried to move her legs, but thick brown mud held her down, pulling her closer and closer to a black spinning hole. She had to get through the swamp, but she couldn't pull herself up to run to the place where she knew she'd be safe. Connor was waiting there. Waiting for her, his hand outstretched.

"Josie?"

She came awake, the sound of his voice calling to her in her dream merging with his gentle whisper.

He was standing over her with coffee and leftover crème brûlée. "I thought you might be hungry."

Josie sat up and looked for her watch. Seven o'clock on Sunday morning. Had it really been only a few days since this nightmare had begun?

She took the coffee but shook her head at the rich, creamy concoction in the ramekin dish. "Thank you."

"I can make toast."

She drank the coffee, willing herself to wake up. "I'm fine. Not hungry." Setting the cup on the glass side table, she whirled off the bed and stood. "I need to get to work. I want to talk to Louis Armond."

"I'm going with you."

She glared up at Connor, shaking her head again. He looked sleep-tossed, too. His dark hair was mushed and messy but his eyes seemed to see everything she needed to hide. "No. You need to stay here and stay out of sight. I have to do this on my own, Connor."

He shoved the tray onto the bed and followed her as she paced in front of the window. "Why? Because you don't trust me? Because I withheld information? Josie, that stuff about the other son is just a hunch."

"We've gone out on less," she retorted. "I wanted to trust you and believe you and cheer you on, but you should have divulged everything

211

up front. Everything. That's how I do my job. I get all the facts and then I use those facts to make a case. I've got nothing, Connor. Nothing."

He turned her to face him. "It's too dangerous for you to go anywhere alone. Don't you see? Whoever this is wants me dead and . . . because you've been seen with me and they know you're FBI, they want you dead, too."

"I'm always on someone's list," she retorted. "I can get Armond to talk, to tell us what was so urgent the night he called you to meet him. I should have had first crack at him anyway, but I abided by my supervisor's orders."

"What makes you think he'll talk to you?"

"I don't know. Maybe because I tried to help him. Maybe because deep down, he respects you?"

"And that matters to you?"

She couldn't deny her feelings but she could put up a wall to protect herself. "Keeping you safe and alive matters to me because it's my job. But you need to be completely honest with me, and . . . you weren't. I can't get past that." She set down her empty coffee cup and started toward the bathroom. "I'm going to headquarters to file my reports and then I'm going to call Sherwood to ask him to take me to see Armond."

"Without me?"

"Yes." She forced herself to ignore the wounded expression in his eyes. "Yes. You can stay here and think back over everything, maybe do more digging on anything that might trigger a memory regarding Armond and his secrets."

"How will you get there?"

She certainly wouldn't hitch a ride in Armond's souped-up car. "I'll call an FBI escort. No problem."

His expression hardened while he stood there staring at her. "Why are you so stubborn?"

"This has nothing to do with me being stubborn," she replied. "We need some time apart, Connor. This situation has brought us together, but if I can't count on you, then I need to investigate this for myself."

"I thought we were a team."

"You thought wrong." She hated seeing him like this—defeated, dangerous—but she had to guard her own heart, and her job. "I'm just the person who's supposed to keep you alive."

"For information, you mean. For the FBI—at your beck and call?"

"Isn't that what you signed up for?"

He nodded, stared out the window. "Yep, I guess so. I sure didn't sign up for this—worrying about you, trying to show you I care, trying to convince you to work with me and not against me."

"I could say the same about you."

She waited for him to leave so she could get ready. But before he did, she turned back. "A young girl died. In Dallas. She was one of my informants, and she was terrified about going in wearing a wire. I told her I'd keep her safe. We set up a sting, but we didn't know that a drug dealer had his own informants in the neighborhood. They found out she'd been spying and they tortured her and murdered her. Her body was there when we raided their meth lab. They were all gone, but they left me a definite message."

Josie sucked in a breath and leaned her head against the bathroom wall. "This job is not easy, but I'd never seen anything like that. It was horrible, and for a while I think I lost my grip on reality." She lifted her head to stare over at him. "Whether you've gone legit or not, I can't have your death on my head. Not after what I've just been through. I can't have you lying or withholding information, either. I need to know every thread, every thought, every move, so I can make the right call."

The look of compassion in his eyes held her. "Josie, I know how this works. I'm always careful. I want to do the right thing, too."

"We all want to do the right thing," she replied. "But sometimes, even that is not enough. I just need you to be honest with me. That's what I need right now."

"I'm not schooled in being honest," he admitted, his head down. "You're . . . you're new territory." He started toward her, then stopped.

"Maybe I'm waiting for the right time, a time when *I* know I can trust *you*."

"We befriend and betray in this job," she said. "Neither of us can pin our hopes on the future, Connor. We can only rely on each other right now, in the moment."

Connor didn't speak. He came over to her and pulled her into his arms. "I'm not a teenager, Josie. I've been at this for most of my life. You can rely on me, no matter what."

She stepped back to touch a hand to his face. "But aren't you tired? Aren't you weary of always having to be on the run, of always looking back to make sure you won't wind up dead in a ditch or left in pieces in the swamp?"

Connor tugged her close again. "I'm completely weary. I want to be the kind of man my sister can respect and admire. I want you to understand me and know I'll always have your back. I want to be a faithful, good man."

"You don't have to prove anything to me," she said, her heart bursting with a feeling she couldn't put a name to. "You only need to prove it to your-self. You have to want it badly enough to make it happen, and that means you have to be open with me."

"I'm trying to come clean," he said, frustration deepening his words. "I need to see this through to the end, this thing with Armond."

"And I need you to give me some space," she

215

replied. "Just for today, just for a little while. I'll get in touch with you as soon as I know something."

Connor didn't believe her. She was angry and disillusioned, and in her mind, he'd failed her. And maybe she was right. He had failed to be completely honest with her, but he had no way of proving his suspicions regarding Armond and the possibility of a secret son. He just went with his gut on these things.

But this time, his gut instincts weren't helping very much.

Except when it came to Josie. He couldn't let her finish this without him. He had a vested interest in ending Armond's long-standing criminal reign but he had another, more important reason, too.

He had to protect Josie, at all costs.

So while he waited for her to get dressed, he sat with another cup of coffee and went back over his notes. Had he seen anything unusual while working with Armond? Anything that could give them a hint on what the man had wanted to tell him that night? Had Armond been ready to turn or had he been trying to warn Connor?

He thought about his time embedded at the Armond mansion. He'd made his way into that shady world by pretending to be a crooked art dealer. He'd conned Armond by fencing several rare pieces—coins, paintings and relics that belonged in museums or with the descendants of the original owners.

He'd helped Armond find the Benoits and was as surprised as everyone else when Armond's papers proved that he did indeed own the three priceless paintings. Primitives of the early Acadians in Louisiana, mixed in with a dreamy kind of real arcadia.

What else?

Pictures. He'd taken pictures, mostly of documents and mostly with a tiny camera that he hid away whenever he had to pass through scanners or stand through being frisked. Most of the pictures hadn't yielded anything concrete. But he had turned in a few to the FBI so they could slowly build a case against Armond.

Connor grabbed his laptop and pulled up the picture files he'd saved from the originals. Just in case. He couldn't think of a better time to revisit those shots. Maybe he'd find something to give him a clue. He planned to go after Josie, but he wanted to take something significant with him when he did.

Josie called Sherwood from her bedroom to let him know she was on her way to the office.

"Gilbert, it's Sunday. You're supposed to be resting until tomorrow."

"I'm fine, sir. Just going into the office to file

217

some reports from my notes." She peeked through the bedroom door to see where Connor was. Still across the big open room, poring over files. "I called for a car. I needed a ride."

"Okay, so that's good. Where's your sidekick?"

"He's going to stay at his apartment. I wanted some time alone to think this through."

"Understandable. Should I put a man on him, just to ease your mind? If you tell me where you are . . ."

"He's locked in tight. Good security. And he can take care of himself."

"So you've seen the real Connor Randall at last?"

Surprised at the venomous tone of that observation, Josie cleared her throat. "I've seen enough to know he's caught up in something he'd like to be done with. But . . . I can't quite trust him. Anyway, I'll check on him once I'm done at the office. Oh, and the reason I called. I need to speak to Armond."

"Negative." Sherwood let out a breath. "I told you he's not talking, and his location is classified for his safety and for yours. He's doing fine. Recovering from his wounds. I think by the time he's able to go home, he'll also be ready to cop a plea and give us anything we want."

"And what about Lou and Vanessa?" She wanted to question both of them again, too.

"They're in town at the Armond apartment.

We've got guards watching them day and night."

"Have they seen Armond?"

"Briefly. Look, I've got to go, but you go in and get your work caught up. Let me handle Armond."

Josie wasn't going away that easily. "If you just give me five minutes with him, I might be able—"

"No, Gilbert. And that's an order."

The call ended before she could respond. She didn't even get to tell him about Connor's suspicions regarding the other son.

"What is going on?" she mumbled, her mind whirling with unanswered questions. She'd take care of her files, pull up more background information and ask around.

But one question stood out in her mind. Why was Sherwood keeping her away from Armond?

Connor waited for Josie to leave. He pretended to be busy, so he scrolled through his file of secret pictures. No one knew he had these, not even the FBI. But then, there'd been nothing of interest in this file, and no one other than the FBI knew he lived in this dilapidated old warehouse. He'd only kept the pictures as insurance in case he ever needed to get reacquainted with all things Armond. He'd kept the laptop hidden in a small space behind a mock cabinet. Not even the cleaning lady knew the files were here.

Josie emerged, fresh-faced and buttoned up. "I

called another agent. He'll park down the street two blocks so he won't bring attention to your apartment."

Connor nodded. "Thanks. This place is pretty hidden and I'd like to keep it that way."

She nodded. "I'm going. I'll call in after I get there."

"Good idea." He got up and followed her to the elevator door. "Be careful, Gilbert. Call me with a fail-safe if you need me."

"Easter Bunny?" Her smile was full of sarcasm.

"How about Cupid?" His thoughts were full of hope. "And only you and I will know it means Help."

"Cupid it is."

He put her on the elevator, then checked all the building monitors to make sure no one was lurking about. But he couldn't stop there, so he went down the elevator and tailed her on foot for two blocks. When he saw the official black SUV, he breathed a sigh of relief and watched her get into the back of the vehicle. Then he went back to his work to finish up so he could follow her and make it to the FBI building just behind her.

Checking his watch, he hurried through the picture files. Nothing. Just Armond conducting business—in a legitimate way most days. Then Armond in a rare moment with his son at a Christmas gathering.

Connor studied one picture. Armond was

laughing with Vanessa as they watched their son opening presents on Christmas Eve. That had been over two years ago. Lou rarely came home, but they'd all been in good moods that year. Connor had been invited to share dinner with them but he'd stayed out of the way while they opened presents.

He did remember the hostile glances Lou had given him that night. But other people had been at that dinner, too.

It struck Connor as odd that criminals could even have such loving, common moments while all the time they were destroying lives and bullying people into doing their bidding.

He was about to move on to the next shot when he noticed something else in the family picture.

Armond was wearing an open shirt that showed a gold coin dangling from an intricate necklace.

Connor lifted his hand to the chain he was still wearing. A chain that looked almost exactly like the one in the picture. Taking the necklace off, he stared down at it.

"Is this what you wanted me to find?" he said out loud. All things considered, this coin necklace had seemed insignificant. But then, everything became important when something became hidden.

Armond had told Beaux to look in the garage. Connor and Josie had found the old garage with the Camaro in it. And Connor had found this coin dangling there. Coincidence? Or had Armond left this for Connor to find?

He studied the engraved coin, flipping it over and over in his fingers. A figure of a woman was etched in the gold. What did this mean? The chain was held to the coin with what looked like a tiny nail drilled into the actual gold. Drilled into the thickness of the coin, not into the top of the coin.

Connor got a jewelry loupe and studied the coin up close. Very old and foreign, or at least it looked like an Italian or Spanish coin. Maybe from some sort of Spanish galleon?

He kept flipping it back and forth, forgetting the time for a few more minutes. When he looked at the clock, he realized more than fifteen minutes had passed since Josie had left.

Had he given her enough time? He didn't want either Josie or Sherwood to know he was tailing her, so he put the coin back around his neck, anxious to tell Josie he thought he'd found what everyone might be looking for.

If this coin was authentic and if there were more where this one had come from, the Armond family could add even more millions to its coffers.

But was this one coin worth killing for?

SEVENTEEN . . .

Josie lifted one booted foot up and into the SUV, then slid inside. Only to find her superior waiting for her.

"Hello, Agent Gilbert."

"Sir?"

Sherwood sat across from her in the dark-windowed vehicle.

Surprised to see him, she glanced around. Other than the driver, they were alone. "Is something up?" she asked, her stomach tightening.

"You wanted to visit with Louis Armond," Sherwood replied, "so I thought I'd take you to him."

"Really?" Glad for this change of plans, Josie had to wonder what had made her superior change his mind. "Is he awake now?"

"He's awake. But sedated."

Josie took in that bit of information, her eyes on the road. "Which hospital?"

Sherwood shifted on the seat. "He's not in a hospital. Too risky. We have him in a secure location."

Shocked, Josie sat up in the seat. When she'd called the service for a driver, she'd instructed him to park down the street from Connor's building and she'd walked to meet him. She didn't want anyone getting too close. Now she had a feeling her SAC had purposely allowed Connor to bring her here.

What else had Sherwood kept from her?

She decided she'd had enough of people holding back on her. "Why haven't you kept me informed on any of this, sir?"

Sherwood gave her a patronizing stare. "I told you I was trying to protect you and your CI."

"Connor seems capable of taking care of himself," she responded, that sick feeling still roiling through her stomach. "And I'm doing okay."

"You two together—now, that's an interesting piece of work."

She watched the roads. She'd been in New Orleans long enough to know they were headed east on I-10. Where had Sherwood hidden Louis Armond?

"Where is Armond?" she asked again.

"You'll know when we get there."

What kind of answer was that? So Sherwood had reconsidered after all, but he still wouldn't disclose the location.

This man whom she'd trusted as her superior had been holding out on her just like Connor. Did they both think she was such a ninny that she couldn't handle the truth that was staring her in the eyes?

"You don't trust me, do you?"

Sherwood shrugged. "You're new and . . . damaged, Gilbert. This is a big case. I've been trying to pin down Louis Armond for most of my career. I'm not about to let a rookie or a known criminal take credit for what I've been trying to do for years."

Josie refused to show any fear or dread. And she couldn't let him see her suspicions, either. "That's your call, sir."

"Yes, it is. Good of you to remember that."

This man wasn't going to tell her anything, so she started memorizing the road signs. They were headed east toward the Lake Pontchartrain Bridge. But they didn't take the bridge exit.

Josie's stomach roiled again. Sherwood didn't say anything more. The silence allowed her to make a mental chart of the man she'd so blindly followed. The man who was nothing short of a control freak. Was Sherwood bitter because Louis Armond had bonded with Connor and then turned to her for help? Because she and Connor had grown close? Did he think she'd purposely tried to take over this case?

Did she dare call Connor?

No. If she got him involved, Sherwood might not let her see Armond. Pushing away her concerns, she tried to engage Sherwood once again. "Remind me of how long you've been after Armond?"

"You don't need to worry about that."

Josie's gut burned with the certain knowledge that Armond might not be waiting for her at the end of this trip. But who would be there? Lou? The alleged other son? Or maybe the silent partner they were all trying to find? Or was Sherwood taking her someplace where she'd never be found? She prepared herself for a long ride. And she prepared herself for a good fight.

Connor took the trolley as far as he could go, then grabbed a cab to the FBI building. After he'd asked the driver to stop a block away, he'd walked by the building twice. Finally, he back-tracked down the street and did a zigzag walk back to the building, making sure no one had followed him. He went to the back entrance. When his key card didn't work, he stood there staring up at the door.

No way he could break in.

So he tried calling Josie. When she didn't answer, Connor got concerned. He remembered she was supposed to text him that she'd made it here okay.

He tried texting her. But after a couple of minutes had passed and she hadn't answered, he turned to leave. Then he tried calling Sherwood.

"I've been waiting for you," Sherwood said after the first ring. "Or should I say we've been waiting for you?"

"Waiting? For what?" Connor didn't like the man's cool, smug tone.

"Actually, I've been waiting for this day for years now," Sherwood replied. "I need you to do me a favor, Randall."

Sure now that Sherwood had Josie, Connor went into his own survival mode. He remembered Josie telling him to think like a criminal. He'd start with a little negotiating. "What do you want, Sherwood?"

Sherwood's laughter sounded with an eerie echo in his ear. "I want you to turn yourself in to the FBI, of course. I want you to confess you've been working with Armond for close to two years now."

"You know I have."

"I know you've pretended to be gathering evidence, and you did manage to give us a nibble here and there, but I want you to confess that you set up that bomb and you planted that evidence in Louis Armond's safe."

Connor closed his eyes, his heartbeat pumping a warning throughout his system. "I didn't do that, and I'm pretty sure you know who did."

"But you'll confess that *you* did."

"Or?"

"Or I might have to put a bullet through Special Agent Josie Gilbert's pretty head."

Josie sat in a dark room, the only sound the drumming of her pulse in her ears. They'd put a blindfold over her eyes so she couldn't see where they were going, but she's sniffed the odors of decay and dampness when they'd hauled her out of the SUV. She thought she'd heard the rocking of a boat hitting a dock, but once they were inside the building, everything went silent. Were they somewhere in the swamp?

The door opened with a creak and a groan. Industrial, maybe? An old warehouse or maybe even a barge on the water.

Sherwood lifted the blindfold away. "How you doing, kid?"

Josie lifted her head in stubborn defiance. She wouldn't go down easy. "I'm fine, sir. Why all the intrigue?"

His chair scraped across concrete. Then he let out a long sigh. "I think you know the answer to that."

"Not really. What I know is that I was trying to do my job and I followed orders to bring in Louis Armond."

"Yep, you did do that. But then something went wrong and you had to go all rogue on me with the dashing Connor Randall."

"Rogue?" Josie wanted to scream. "We did not go rogue. We went on the run because someone was also after us and you told us to stay hidden. Whoever shot Lewanna also wants Armond and the two of us dead."

She didn't add that she'd pretty much figured

out who that someone was. But she had to ask. "Did you instruct me to stay hidden so *you* could get to Armond?"

"You're a smart woman. What do you think?"

Josie didn't know what to think at this point. "None of this makes any sense to me, sir. I trusted you and I trusted Connor. That's part of my job —to put my trust in my superiors and to put my trust in my informants. I tried to do that. What did I miss?"

"What did you miss?" Sherwood's voice grew louder with each word. "You missed an opportunity to take down Louis Armond. You had him, Gilbert. Had him right there, ready to turn. But you blew it by helping Connor to hide the old man."

"We did everything to save him so he could talk to us," she countered. "We brought him to you—"

Josie stopped, sucked in a breath. "We brought him right to you."

"Now you're beginning to see things in a whole new light. You did do the right thing, Gilbert. But I can't get past some of the things you and Randall didn't do."

Josie wanted to play dumb, but her fate was sealed. No one would ever find her. She knew it and she accepted it but she wouldn't give in to it. "Did you set up the explosion and that bogus evidence in Armond's bedroom and the shoot-out at the hotel?"

"Maybe."

She could see his smug smile. Knowing he'd betrayed her and the organization they'd both pledged to serve, Josie felt sick to her stomach. "Was it that important that you bring down Armond? Sir, we had him. You said it yourself. You could have taken him in and locked him up."

Tapping his fingers on the table, Sherwood moved closer. "And for how long? Until he lawyers up and gets away with murder again?"

"Murder?" Josie's heart pumped so fast, she thought she'd pass out. "What do you mean, murder?"

The room went deadly still. Then Sherwood hissed another breath. "You don't need to worry about that, Gilbert."

"Then why am I here?"

"You're here because you got too close."

"To Connor, to Armond, or to the truth?"

"The truth has always been right there," Sherwood replied. "It took me a long time to piece it all together, but I had it all figured out. Then two things happened. Instead of killing him, Armond developed a fondness for Connor Randall and . . . then you showed up."

"So Connor and I have to pay for that?"

"Not pay so much as suffer. You both got in the way of something I need. But I've found a way to get rid of Randall—finally."

Josie couldn't imagine what that might be

unless he planned to kill Connor. But then her head started spinning with what she knew about this case.

"Everyone seems to want something that they can't find," she said. "What have you done with Lou Junior and Vanessa?"

He stared down his nose at her. "They are safe. They both have alibis for the night of the bomb explosion, so I can't pin much on them."

She didn't believe that. "Did you start the fire, too?"

"I'm the one doing the interrogating here, Gilbert."

She'd take that as affirmative. He must have been the shadow she'd seen on the stairs. "I wonder what all the fuss is about. What was in that garage?"

"You need to stop working and relax," Sherwood said.

"What are you planning to do with me?" Josie retorted, her nerves twitching. She breathed in and out and told herself to stay calm. She might still be a rookie in this man's eyes, but she wouldn't sit here all meek and mild and let him intimidate her. He'd lost that right when he'd kidnapped her. Or maybe way before then, if she'd only seen the truth.

Connor tried to warn you.

Connor.

"What have you done with Connor, sir?"

Sherwood's chuckle hit the still, hot air. "Oh, him? Well, I hate to tell you this, Gilbert. But your man Randall is probably on his way here right now."

"What do you mean?"

"He confessed to being in cahoots with Louis Armond."

"I don't believe you."

"I don't care what you believe. He confessed to me over the phone earlier. I think he's the one who planted that bomb and that phony evidence we found."

"Then why bring him here? Shouldn't you turn him in to someone at headquarters?"

"I won't be turning him in just yet. Maybe never. First he has to confess to what he's known all along."

Josie's heart lurched to a stop. She'd trust Connor any day over this madman. But now it was too late for that. She might not ever be able to see Connor again. She'd be dead soon and Connor would be framed for crimes he didn't commit.

But if she kept Sherwood talking, maybe she'd finally find out the truth. "And what's that?"

"He knew what was in that garage. He also knew what was in that rickety old barn where the hidden car was located. In fact, I'm pretty sure he's been in cahoots with Louis Armond for years now. I knew I couldn't trust him, and now I can prove it. He did what a criminal always does, Gilbert. He played all of us."

"You need to explain," she replied, holding out hope while she prayed that Connor was still alive.

"No need for me to explain."

The chair scraped across the floor again.

"He should be arriving here any minute. And when he gets here, you can be a witness to his confession. Not that it will matter much after today." Sherwood leaned so close she could smell the stale coffee on his breath.

"After he confesses and I get what I need, you will both be useless to me."

Josie knew what that meant. He would never let either of them see the light of day again.

EIGHTEEN . . .

Sherwood left the room.

Josie gave up on staying quiet and safe. He'd tied her hands behind her with a loose rope, but she'd already been working on that before he'd come into the room. With a little more twisting, she had the rope loosened enough to maneuver her right hand free. While she worked the ropes so she could make them look as if they were still tied, she studied her surroundings. The room was industrial, stark and empty, cold and damp, with only one door out. She got up and ran to the door, only to find it locked. No windows, no two-way mirrors. She glanced up at the ceiling. No cameras?

She thought about what he'd told her. Connor turning himself in, admitting he'd been working with Armond instead of against him, keeping her hidden away so she couldn't question Armond. It made no sense. Connor had protected her, saved her, and he'd kept her on the run.

At whose request? Sherwood had agreed they both needed to stay hidden. Had he manipulated both of them?

Now she doubted everything and everyone. But she would take matters into her own hands from here on out.

If Sherwood had Armond hidden, Connor might know that and he might come after Sherwood whether he was on Armond's side or not. She had to get a message to Connor.

Turning back to the tiny desk near where she'd been sitting, she noticed a landline telephone. Dust covered it but the wireless receiver sat inside a charger that was plugged into the wall.

Glancing at the door, Josie took a chance. She grabbed the receiver and prayed for a dial tone. When she heard one, she quickly dialed Connor's cell number and waited. When she only got his voice message, her heart sank. Then she heard a voice outside the room, someone talking, maybe into a phone. Sherwood coming back?

Josie watched the door while she waited for the beep to leave a message, her breath counting the precious seconds. The beep sounded. The door lock rattled and clicked. She said one word before she placed the phone back in its cradle and rushed back to her chair. "Cupid."

Cupid.

Their fail-safe code.

Connor hurried down side streets and listened, his throat clogging with pain and fear.

And anger.

Sherwood had taken her, and now Sherwood expected Connor to take the rap for *his* wrong-doings. Turn himself in and confess to deeds Sherwood had obviously perpetrated?

No way.

But he said he'd kill Josie.

Connor called Sherwood back and dangled a carrot in front of him.

"Before you starting doling out ultimatums, Sherwood, I found something that you might be interested in."

"I'm only interested in sending you and Louis Armond to prison," Sherwood retorted. "It's too late, Randall. I've got agents in place to escort you back to headquarters. When you get there, you will confess to being a double agent. You worked for Armond and I've got evidence to back up my suspicions."

"Evidence that you produced?"

"Evidence that you so readily provided, but nothing that I could use to stick it to him. You were careful, smart, unshakable. I had to doctor things up. Well, now you'll pay for your little games."

Connor wouldn't let this man rattle him. "I'm thinking you've managed to plant evidence, Sherwood. That's what you did the night of the explosion, right?" He skipped a beat, then added, "Or how about evidence that will prove you're Armond's silent partner?"

"You'll never get anyone to believe that," Sherwood said, anger escaping with a hiss.

So, that was it, then. FBI Special Agent in Charge Joseph Sherwood was notorious Mafia king Louis Armond's silent partner.

Connor knew he'd never beat the rap, but he could try to save Josie. "This is between you and me now, and I can show you what I've found. I think I have the real evidence—against you—and that's why you've been keeping Armond hidden, and that's why you've been trying to kill Josie and me. You thought we already had the evidence, thought maybe Armond had given it to us that night we helped him. Let her go. She knows nothing about your true identity and we can keep it that way."

Sherwood let out a curse. "Not so fast. She's in the middle of it, and she showed her loyalties when she ran away with you."

"You gave her permission to do so. Did you expect her to leave me hanging? Is that why you're so angry?"

"I expected her to do her job and bring you both in, but you talked her into running and taking that washed-up crime boss with you."

The rage in those words sent a chill down Connor's spine. If Sherwood had been working double time with Armond all these years, he'd do anything to protect himself. Including killing as many people as he possibly could.

"Listen, I have a coin," Connor finally blurted. "I think I know how to break it open. And I think I know what's inside. Probably a SIM card or some sort of thumb drive. Interested? Or should I just give it to the locals?"

The line went silent for a minute. "You're smarter than I gave you credit for," Sherwood hissed. "You're running out of time, though. You've got two hours to leave the coin in a place of my choosing. If you don't show up, the woman's dead. And Armond will have to die, too. The next time you hear of Josie Gilbert, it will be on the evening news. Her body will be floating in the swamp right next to his. Or what's left of them."

Connor swallowed the bile in his throat. "What do you want me to do?"

Sherwood named a spot in City Park where he wanted Connor to bring the coin.

"Don't try anything, Randall. I have her and I'll keep her here until I've got that coin."

Connor wasn't stupid. "You can't have the coin until I see Josie. If you do anything to harm her before I can see her and we can make the exchange, I'll take what I have right to the FBI."

"My people won't believe you."

"I won't take it to your people here in New Orleans. I'll take it all the way to Washington, D.C."

Sherwood only hesitated a minute. "You'll see your precious Josie as long as I get the coin."

After Sherwood ended the call, Connor started running back toward his apartment. He only had a little while to get home and prepare himself for confronting Sherwood. The man would shoot him on the spot in the park and then he'd kill Josie and Armond and somehow make it look as if Connor had done it. They'd all be dead and the real criminal would get away free and clear.

With that scenario running through his brain, Connor sprinted around corners and hurried through alleyways.

Then his phone buzzed an incoming message he'd missed while talking to Sherwood. Connor hit the screen to retrieve the message. From Josie.

Cupid.

Connor heard the resolve and the urgency in her

voice. Did she think she'd never see him again? That he would run and leave her in the hands of a madman who'd convinced her that Connor was the bad guy? Did she know that he'd do anything to save her? Anything.

Connor increased his speed. He had to find out where the call had come from. He started to work right away, sending out signals to his street contacts as he jogged the sidewalks. He described the vehicle he'd watched driving away, even gave them the license-plate numbers he'd memorized. Then he checked his phone to see if the number she'd called from had come through.

It had. So he called a friend at the telephone company and begged her to break all the rules to track down the phone number by doing a reverse search. After telling her this was urgent, he said, "It's a local, but I can't get a handle on where it might be and I'm running out of time."

"If it's a cell, it's gonna be hard to pin down," she explained. "Let me see what I can come up with."

He hurried back to his place and started gathering the tools he'd need to go after Sherwood. A Glock 22 with extra ammo, a hunting knife, a flashlight and a camera, and a bungee cord. He'd learned a few things about weaponry and espionage while hanging around with the FBI and Armond.

He put everything but his cell phone into a

black canvas backpack and waited for his friend to call back.

After ten minutes and a bucket of sweat, his cell rang.

"It's a landline at an old abandoned manufacturing company northwest of the city, near Lake Pontchartrain's south shore."

Connor memorized the address and started out the door. This place was located in a wetland village out from the city. A place where a person could go missing for a very long time.

An image of Josie floating in the brackish waters of a shallow swamp hit him. Connor closed his eyes and said a silent prayer. "Don't let her die because of my sins, Lord."

Then he hit numbers on his phone as he moved through the New Orleans streets. "Mama Joe, it's Connor. I need your help."

Josie was back in the chair with her hands behind her back before Sherwood closed the door. Trying to steady her breath, she stared up at him.

Sherwood came around the table and looked at her hands.

Josie held her breath while he made sure she was still tied. She'd done her best to make it look that way.

"Your ropes look loose," Sherwood said. Then he yanked at the cords with such force, Josie had to grit her teeth against the burning scrape of

240

skin being torn off her wrists. "But you can't get out of this building. It's airtight and out in the middle of nowhere." He leaned close, his smile belying his words. "And surrounded by big, hungry gators."

Josie refused to let him scare her. "Thanks for the warning."

Sherwood stood tall and rocked back on his heels. "I had a nice chat with your partner in crime."

"Connor?"

She hated the plea in that question. Sherwood would use it against her.

"Yes, Connor. Charming, conniving, conflicted Connor. He's trying to make a deal."

Josie wouldn't let this man convince her that Connor wasn't doing everything in his power to help her. "I'd expect no less."

"So you know him and don't even care that he's still a criminal?"

"I know him and I believe he's trying to change. That he will change for the good."

"Amazing." Sherwood paced in front of the old desk. "I've decided to bring him out here to our little party."

She swallowed, prayed that Connor would get away. "No need for that, right? I mean, if he confesses, you're free and clear. I hope you've built a good case against him. Covered all of your tracks." She settled back against her chair, willing herself to stay calm. "Exactly how long have you been Armond's silent partner, anyway?"

Sherwood whirled and pounced, his fingers digging into her shoulders as he lifted her out of the chair. "You have no idea what you're talking about."

She stared at him, the courage of a last resort giving her strength. "I think I do know what I'm talking about. I think each time Connor got too close, you pulled him back just enough to make it look like he wasn't doing his job. I think you insisted he back off after the Benoit fiasco last year because he was very close to finding out the truth—that you're the one who's been working with Armond for years now."

She shrugged away from his grasp. "It was almost the perfect cover. Until I showed up."

"Until Connor Randall showed up," Sherwood replied. "Did he ever tell you how he got that fancy loft apartment?"

She had to admit to herself she'd wondered about Connor's explanation regarding the loft, but she wouldn't give Sherwood the satisfaction of knowing that. "His mother left it. But I'm not worried about that."

"Oh, you should be," Sherwood retorted, his hand moving over his close-shaved hair. "But I won't spoil the surprise. I'll wait and let him explain all of this to you himself."

Josie held a breath. "You won't find him."

"I don't have to find him," Sherwood replied. "He's agreed to meet me and . . . he doesn't know it yet, but he'll have to turn himself in and come with me if he ever wants to see you alive again."

NINETEEN . . .

Before he left for the Carousel Gardens in City Park, Connor tried to open the coin. He'd realized after looking at the slender pin that held the coin to the necklace that this silver-dollar-size gold coin was similar to the coins spies used back in the day before electronics took over. It was an old-school piece and probably worth a lot of money on its own merit.

But whatever was inside might be worth more than gold. The coin was big enough to hold a wealth of information on a tiny SIM card or thumb drive. Connor casily manipulated the pin by turning it until the coin clicked open. He didn't have time to look at the information, but he did find what he'd expected.

A little flat black card that should fit in a smartphone or a computer. Armond had pretended he didn't know or care about electronics, but he'd been smart enough to hide this information on a small electronic device. This little inch-square file could tell the tale on all of Armond's operations, including the identity of his very silent and now very scared partner. Information that would probably point to Joseph Sherwood as being the person everyone had been looking for—right there in plain sight for years now.

When Connor thought back over his time with Armond, he could see it all now. Each time he'd bring a solid report to the FBI, Sherwood would somehow decide it wasn't enough. Or evidence would suddenly go missing so Connor had no proof of his observations. Not enough probable cause or not enough to get a search warrant, so many tiny rules that always caused the FBI to back off. Sherwood had been going behind him with each assessment, changing facts and destroying evidence.

Who was the real con man here now?

Armond must have decided he couldn't do it anymore. He'd called the one person he felt he could trust—Connor.

Had he wanted Connor and Josie to find this? Or maybe he'd hoped his son would find it and give up the goods on Sherwood. This had to have been what Vanessa and Lou had been so eager to find that night of the garage fire. But did they want to help Louis or just destroy his will and maybe what would be his confession?

Connor carefully took the tiny card out of the coin and stored it in a safe place in his backpack.

Then he replaced the card with an old one from one of his phones. It would look like the real deal long enough to buy him some time.

By the time Sherwood figured out he'd been duped, Connor hoped to be on his way out of the country with Josie. He didn't stop to think about whether she'd be willing to go with him or not. He just headed out on instincts and hope.

Right now, he had to get to the park and make the switch.

"Can I see Armond now?"

Josie wondered where Sherwood was taking her. He'd hinted they might go for a little ride. Would it be her last ride or was he moving her to throw off Connor?

"Sure," her corrupt supervisor retorted. "You'll get to see everybody before this is over."

"Everybody? What do you mean?"

"You ask way too many questions, Gilbert. Should have left you in Dallas."

"Why did you hire me?" she asked, thinking he'd used her mistakes against her.

Sherwood took her down a long hallway. "I figured you had a grudge against the Connor Randall type, considering your old man was one of the most notorious white-collar criminals in the Lone Star State."

"Why don't we leave my father out of this?"

"Still eats at you, doesn't it? You with your

perfect scores and stellar performance. Your crooked daddy's the driving force behind your code of honor. But even your strong sense of duty didn't keep you from messing up in Dallas, did it?"

Josie allowed him to shove her along, but she noted each hall crossing and exit sign as they went. The lighting system was low and weak but she could tell this place was like a maze. A musky gray maze she might not ever escape.

"What? No comeback, Gilbert? I'm disappointed in you."

"You thought you could just dole out petty assignments to me, give me enough cases to keep me hopping while you kept right on working with Armond. But you misjudged all of us. You probably enjoyed shoving me toward Connor."

"Oh, yeah. I knew he'd charm his way into your straitlaced system. Was I wrong on that?"

"He's a charmer, that's for sure," Josie retorted, remembering Connor's kisses. "But he's nobody's fool. He's got you figured out, so I'd say you're the one who should be worried right now."

"Shut up," Sherwood said, his voice rasping like a burning wire against her skin. "Just shut up. You'll see the real Connor Randall. Finally."

"I hope so," Josie said. She hoped she'd see Connor again. She prayed he'd stay safe and stay smart.

When Sherwood opened a door, she fully

expected to find Connor there waiting for her. But the man lying bloody and tied to the bed wasn't Connor.

Louis Armond moaned and opened his eyes. "Who's there?"

Sherwood laughed. "Hey, Armond, since you were so willing to double-cross me, I brought you some company. To take on the journey with you when I throw you into the swamp."

Armond moaned again and glanced up. When he saw Josie, he pulled at his restraints. "Where's my son? What have they done with my son?"

Connor waited by the carousel, checking his watch to make sure he was on time. His heart ticked off the seconds, every one precious until he had Josie in his arms again.

Imagine him falling for an FBI agent? He shook his head as memories swirled and twirled like the painted horses going around and around on the carousel. Children's laughter echoed around the musical ride, reminding Connor of things he'd tried to forget.

He'd never planned on falling in love. Who'd want a man like him anyway? He was damaged, broken, bitter and ruthless.

Would Josie want him?

The Lord wants you.

His sister's gentle reminder held him steady. He thought of the thief on the cross next to Jesus.

The Lord had told that man he'd see him in heaven.

Connor closed his eyes and envisioned Josie's always-doubtful smile. "Will I see you in heaven?"

He asked God to allow him a bit more time on earth. Just until he could put the real criminals away forever.

"After that, Lord, I'll leave it in your hands."

When he opened his eyes, he saw a man wearing a dark suit and sunglasses approaching him. Connor prepared for a fight. He wasn't giving up this coin until he saw Josie. Glancing around, he took strength in knowing Mama Joe's men had his back.

The man walked up to a bench a few feet from Connor and sat down to look straight ahead. Connor approached and took a seat next to him.

"Do you have what we need?" the man asked.

"That depends," Connor replied. "Do you have the package I've requested?"

The man glanced around, then turned toward Connor. "If you can't give me what I came for, I'm to take you to meet my supervisor."

Connor nodded, then stood up to give the man a once-over. They were close to the same size and height. "Lead the way."

"I need to take that backpack," the man replied.

"Negative." Connor stood over him. "I have what you want, but I'm not giving it up until I see the woman."

"Then you'll have to take a nice drive with me out into the country."

"I'm prepared to do that," Connor retorted.

That and more. They'd try to take the backpack away from him when he got there, but he hoped before then he'd have help in securing this messenger and some of Mama Joe's boys would be there to get behind the wheel.

Josie rushed to Armond's bed and tried to check him over. "How long have you had him here?"

Armond went in and out of consciousness, still moaning and asking for his family. He tried to reach out to Josie, his hand old and withered, like a broken bit of dry bramble clawing at her skin.

"Tell him where his wife and son are," Josie said, her hand on Armond's arm. "He's worried about his family."

"Relax," Sherwood said, shaking his head. "You do remember he's a criminal, right?"

"I remember everything," she retorted. "But have you forgotten everything we stand for? This man should be in a hospital."

"He was, long enough to save his sorry life. I convinced the hospital personnel to let me take him to a safe place. He agreed to it, since he's so afraid for his life." He shrugged. "Or maybe he's afraid I'll kill someone he really loves."

Armond moaned. "No agreement. Kidnapped."

Sherwood walked up to the bed. "I should have killed you myself, since you can't seem to let go and just die."

Josie wondered why he'd kept Armond alive. "Are you making him suffer because you thought he was going to turn on you?"

"I'm making him suffer because he's a liar and a cheat and I'm tired of fighting the system. We have to walk a tightrope to bring in scum like this. I got tired of all the rules and regulations."

"So you took matters into your own hands?"

Sherwood nodded. "I needed to keep him alive for leverage."

Josie inhaled a deep breath. "So you could lure Connor and me into a trap because you were afraid we'd find out the truth?"

Sherwood nodded, his scowl softening. "I knew sooner or later you'd want to talk to Armond, and I couldn't allow that. That's the FBI way, isn't it? Question everyone and everything? Get the evidence, record and preserve the crime scene. Jump through hoops while these scumbags get away with everything from murder to . . . taking over a man's soul. And so on and so forth."

Josie saw a trace of regret in his wary eyes, but she didn't give Sherwood any points for it. "So you got tired of doing all of that?"

Sherwood let out his own long sigh, his brown eyes going dull. "I'm close to retirement, Gilbert. But a few years ago, I got tired of beating my head against the wall . . . and I made a few bad decisions."

"So you joined up with Armond—to bring him to justice or maybe to pad your retirement funds? Why, Agent Sherwood? Why did you do this?"

Sherwood turned away from the man on the bed. "I got greedy and saw an opportunity too good to pass up."

Josie wondered what made a person take such a risk. "So you're the one who's been helping Armond along all these years, protecting him, warning him. But you tried to pin some of that on Connor, since he kept getting closer and closer to the truth."

"The truth," Sherwood replied with a snarl, "is so well hidden no one could find it." He pointed to Armond. "This man knows where he hid the truth—the fact of the matter is that truth is much bigger than any petty deals I had with Armond. But he's too stupid to tell me or anyone else— even the amazing Connor Randall."

"And that's the only reason you're keeping him alive. You're afraid if he dies, someone will find what he's hidden and you'll be exposed."

Sherwood's chuckle echoed over the still room. "Everyone is looking for something, Gilbert."

"The garage fire—did you set that?"

"No," Sherwood admitted. "I think Little Lou panicked on that one. His mother is so afraid we'll all go to jail, she tried to tear down the

251

place so she could find the hidden evidence."

"You're right on one thing," Josie said, her gaze on Armond. "Everyone is looking for the proof of the criminal activities you and Armond have been involved in for years now." She turned from the man on the bed and stared straight into Sherwood's cold brown eyes. "And you'd better hope none of us found it."

"You'd better hope your boyfriend brings me what I want," Sherwood shouted. "Or I'll kill you and this old man before Randall ever gets to tell you goodbye."

TWENTY . . .

"Sir, he refuses to give us the . . . uh . . . item. He insists on coming out there to meet you."

Connor sat in the backseat of the blacked-out SUV, praying Sherwood wouldn't have him executed on the spot. His real backpack had everything he might need to save Josie but he'd left it with Mama Joe's backup men. The only thing he had on him now was the tiny SIM card that would hopefully clear his name and tell the world the truth about who had been helping Sherwood for years now. He had the real card stashed in a safe place on his person and he'd put the fake one in the coin around his neck to use as a decoy. The empty backpack would also serve as a decoy.

"I can kill him," the big man offered on an enthusiast note.

Connor waited two heartbeats, then blurted, "I have what he wants, but I want to give it to him in person. And only after I see that Josie is alive and unharmed."

The man repeated his statement into the phone. "Fine. We're on our way." He put the phone down and turned to Connor. "Good news, sunshine. You get to live for a little while longer."

"Nice," Connor retorted, sarcasm hiding the urgency of the situation. He only wanted to live long enough to get Josie out of there. But if things worked out the way he hoped, they'd walk out together.

Sherwood would kill all of them. Of that he had no doubt. He'd kill them and make it look as if Connor had been the silent partner who'd mowed them all down then got himself shot in the cross fire.

What would his sister, Deidre, think about that?

He couldn't let them do this to Deidre. Or Josie. Josie didn't deserve this, and she sure didn't deserve to die just because he'd made one too many mistakes.

But he promised himself and God that getting involved with Armond would be his last mistake.

●●●

Josie sat by Armond's dingy bed, wondering what Sherwood planned to do with them. He'd left her here with Armond, but he'd warned her that he had cameras on them. Armond was asleep and cuffed to the bed, so she didn't see how Sherwood expected her to try anything. If she'd heard right, Connor was on his way here. But why? Why hadn't he gone to the FBI and reported Sherwood?

When she thought about that scenario, though, she could understand why Connor hadn't sought help from the authorities. A high-up, well-respected FBI agent versus a confidential informant who had a shady past. Which one would she believe if she didn't know the truth?

She closed her eyes and asked God to forgive her for not seeing the truth that had been right in front of her. But how could any of them have known this? Still wanting to put it all together, she tried to picture Sherwood and Armond working together. It didn't add up, but then she'd had a hard time believing her own father had turned out to be a criminal, too.

Armond moaned and opened his eyes. He glanced over at Josie, surprise making him grunt. "What are you doing here?"

Josie couldn't be sure how coherent he was, so she decided to stick to generalities. "Sherwood brought me here to see you. Is there anything you want to tell me, anything you remember?"

Armond coughed and gave her one of his penetrating stares. "Too many memories. Too much to explain. Where is my son?"

Josie's hands were tied behind her back again, so she couldn't get any closer. "Lou? He and Vanessa are safe." She hoped and prayed. "I think Sherwood has them somewhere in the building." She leaned up in her chair.

Armond became agitated. "Did you find—"

The door opened and Sherwood waltzed in. "Enough chitchat. We're expecting company."

Josie's heart bumped painfully inside her body. "Connor?"

"Miss him, Gilbert?"

"Just concerned," she replied, her tone cool in spite of her quickening pulse. "Do you think you'll actually get away with this?"

"I don't see any problem in getting away with this."

She wanted to shout there were two very strong problems—her and Connor. But her helpless situation tore at her. She could easily escape if she set her mind to it, but she wouldn't leave Armond or Connor. She'd wait until Connor showed up and then maybe together they could figure something out.

When the SUV pulled up to the rusted-out industrial building, Connor tried to see through the blacked-out windows to gauge the building's

255

shape. Long and narrow, two-storied, with very few windows and doors. A maze out in the middle of the swamp. The building was only yards from the lake and tucked back along a narrow dirt road. Probably something to do with shipping, but Connor wondered what kind of shipping.

Not that it mattered right now. Still studying his surroundings, he got out of the truck and breathed in the smells of stale oil and decaying loam. Somewhere off in the dense, mossy woods, an animal hurried through the underbrush. The whole place was enveloped in a mantle of desolation and loneliness.

This was the kind of place where people came to die.

But he didn't plan on dying here. And he sure didn't plan on anybody he loved dying here. "Let's get this over with," he told his guards.

They took him by his elbows and guided him into the main doors. Once the squeaking doors closed behind him, Connor started making plans. His keepers had frisked him, but he'd expected that, so he'd kept his cool and let them have at it. He expected Sherwood to immediately force them to do a more thorough search.

Which was why he'd also asked Mama Joe's boys to bring their own weapons and the one he'd tucked into the backpack. The only thing he had on him now that mattered was the real SIM card. And he'd stashed it in a place the guards wouldn't think to check—inside his bootheel. He could go old-school himself when needed.

The goons pushed him down a long, dark hallway toward another double steel door. This place was about as isolated as you could get, but Connor had brought his own brand of backup for that very reason. Mama Joe's boys could find their way through a maze of live alligators.

When the two men pushed him through the doors, he braced himself for anything and held his breath.

"Welcome." Special Agent Sherwood smiled and motioned Connor inside the long, dark room.

Heat and humidity hung in the stale air like wet curtains. It clogged Connor's throat and dripped down his hair and neck.

He took in the scene, his gaze hitting on Josie first. She was tied to a chair, her hands and feet twisted together with rope.

She gave him an imploring return stare, but what he saw in her eyes gave him the boost he needed to get this over with.

She looked at him in a way that showed she believed in him.

Connor returned that gaze, then moved on. Shocked to see Louis Armond lying unkempt in a dirty hospital bed, he stared at the old man and wondered how he'd survived this long. Then he did a quick appraisal of the rest of the room. Lou Junior and Vanessa sat in a corner, their mouths taped over, their hands and feet tied. They both looked fatigued and terrified.

"Looks like I'm a little late to the party," Connor finally said. He took another quick glance around the room, then rested his gaze on Josie.

When Armond heard his voice, he lifted his head. "Connor, no. Connor, leave."

Sherwood's chuckle cut through the tension hanging over the big room. "No, no. You're right on time, Randall. Or maybe about thirty years too late, depending on who's doing the talking."

Armond grunted again. Sherwood stalked to his bed. "Shut up, old man. I told you you'd regret stepping over that line, but you wouldn't listen to me, would you? You went and got involved with Randall here again, asking him for help. Did you think you'd really get away with that?"

Armond glared up at Sherwood, but he ran out of steam and slumped back against his pillow.

"He looks bad," Connor said in a nonchalant tone. "What'd you do to him, Sherwood?"

Joseph Sherwood turned then, all kidding aside. "You know what I did to the old man, Randall. He tried to double-cross me, so I decided it was time to haul him in, dead or alive."

Vanessa moaned through her taped mouth, her dark eyes flashing fire at Sherwood. He walked over and leaned down in front of her. "I tried to warn you, too, darling. Told you two to stay away, but you were so afraid that everyone would find out the truth, you nearly ruined all of our plans."

Armond's wife gazed up at Joseph Sherwood with a dark plea in her eyes. Then she glared at the man in the bed.

The whole scene was like something out of an opera, Connor decided. All they needed was an orchestra and a soprano.

Connor pushed the issue, his mind whirling with ways to play all the main characters against each other. "So you two were in this together? Is that why you gathered all of us here?"

Sherwood turned around and stalked back to Connor. "You have no idea, none at all, what a hornets' nest you stirred up by agreeing to help this pathetic old man."

Connor cut his gaze to Sherwood. "Why don't you tell me, then?"

"Give me the goods," Sherwood said, grabbing the necklace Connor wore. "Since you're so attached to this, I guess you've got what I need hidden in here somewhere."

Connor halfheartedly pretended to hold on to the gold coin. "No, I told your goons I wouldn't let go of this until I knew Josie was safe."

"And doesn't she look just fine? Comfortable and with a front-row seat to all the action."

"I thought I knew you," Connor retorted. "We all thought we knew you." He glanced back at Josie. The disappointment on her face broke his heart. "You used Agent Gilbert and me, sending us here and there, while you transported Armond and his family out here. Why? For your own kind of justice?"

Sherwood grabbed the necklace again and, with a grunt and a yank, broke it away from Connor's neck.

Connor gritted his teeth against the ripping pain, his raw skin burning with perspiration. But he refused to give Sherwood any satisfaction. "I didn't know you liked gold so much, Sherwood."

Sherwood turned the coin over several times. "What is this? Some kind of a joke? Where is it, Randall?"

"Where's what?" Connor lifted his eyes to meet Josie's, hoping he could convey everything he wanted to say to her.

"You know what," Sherwood shouted, his voice scaring Vanessa Armond into a fit of tears. "She knows what I'm talking about and she's scared, so scared that you've figured things out."

"What's to figure out?" Connor asked, holding his hands up, then dropping them back down. "You tell me what you think I have, Sherwood, and then I'll tell you if I have it."

"Oh, I get it," Sherwood said. He stalked back to Connor and glared at him. "You don't really know what I'm looking for. Are you bluffing me, Randall?"

"No bluff here," Connor said, his nose inches

from Sherwood's. "I have something, but I want to hear you ask for it. It must be really valuable to you."

Sherwood spun around and went for Josie. He grabbed her up out of the chair and held her by the arm, one hand out to stop Connor from coming for him. "Don't even think about it!" he shouted. "I'm done with your games, Randall. Is this information more valuable than this woman?"

"No," Connor replied, his eyes on Josie. He gave her a quick wink and then nodded toward the necklace. "It's inside the coin. There's a small hollow space inside."

Josie let out a gasp of breath. "Did you know that all along?"

"No," Connor replied, his heart pumping a message to her. "I only discovered it a little while ago."

She nodded, her gaze moving from the coin in Sherwood's hand and then back to Connor. He tried to convey the truth to her and then he looked down at his boot, hoping she'd realize he wasn't going to double-cross her.

While Sherwood tried to open the coin, Connor sent a warning glance to Josie. She was back in the chair and settled, but he could tell instead of fearing for her life she was busy calculating how she was going to get them all out of here. Sherwood knew she wouldn't leave without everyone he'd been holding, so he obviously wasn't too concerned about her trying anything. That and the two men with the big guns at the door, of course.

But Connor knew she wouldn't give up. She was that kind of agent. She'd save these people, even though they'd all kill her in a New York minute if the cards were turned.

Staring past the two guards, Connor gave her an imploring glance. He couldn't let her attempt to help him. They'd shoot her just to spite him if he moved.

Sherwood finally motioned to Connor. "Show me how to get into this thing. Now!"

Connor did as he asked, praying Sherwood wouldn't download the whole thing right away. Just a few more minutes . . .

When Connor sprang open the coin and showed Sherwood the tiny square black card, the other man stared at it as if *it* were a piece of gold, then he turned it around and around in his hand. Finally, he turned back to Armond. "I have it now. I have the whole operation right here. And there is nothing any of you can do about it."

Armond lifted up and snarled. In the corner, Vanessa and Lou both tried to talk through their taped mouths. Connor looked from Sherwood to Armond, then to Josie. He sent her a slight shrug, then looked down at his boots again. Would she understand what he was telling her?

Josie leaned close to Armond. "What is it? What are you trying to say?"

Sherwood heard her and rushed to the bed, pushing her back in her chair before he knocked Armond back down. "You're not going to blow this for me now, are you, old friend?"

Armond gained strength, anger coloring his wrinkled, shrunken face. Then he lifted up and stared straight at Connor.

"My son," he said, hatred in his eyes as he cut them back to Sherwood. "That's the real prize that you can't take away. Connor, you are my son."

TWENTY-ONE . . .

The room went still. Vanessa's eyes widened to the point of popping out of her head. Armond's watery gaze held Connor's. Lou dropped his head, his body shaking with either rage or emotion.

Josie sat stunned and flabbergasted, thinking she'd heard wrong. Surely she'd heard wrong. She tore her eyes away from Armond and lifted her head toward Connor. Had he know this all along?

Could she trust anyone?

"What is he talking about?" she asked, her eyes

still on Connor. "Connor, what is he saying?"

Connor stood frozen to the spot, his face ashen and pale. "That's a lie," he finally said. "You're just desperate to say anything to save yourself, Armond."

Louis Armond shifted on the bed, his gaze roving until he centered his eyes on Sherwood. "Tell them," he said. "Tell them everything and . . . let me die in peace."

Sherwood started laughing. "Of course Randall knows. How do you think he got that fancy loft apartment and drove that nice sports car? Think about it, Gilbert. He wasn't shadowing Armond because he wanted justice. He was following his daddy around, hoping for the keys to the kingdom. It's in the will—all of it." He pointed toward Vanessa and Lou. "And these two didn't want that will or any of the Armond company records to be found."

"Neither did you," Armond said on breath that dragged with fatigue. "Neither did you."

Vanessa moaned and tugged at her restraints. Waving his gun in the air, Sherwood marched over to her chair and lifted her up. "Let's let your wife tell the real story, so we'll all understand why I had to do what I did. Let her explain this whole bizarre twist in our circumstances."

Vanessa shook her head, pulling back as if she was going to her execution. And maybe she was. Maybe they all were.

Josie shifted her gaze back to Connor. He shook his head, shock brightening his eyes. How had he not known that the man he'd tried to put away was his own father?

Sherwood ripped the tape off Vanessa's mouth, causing Lou to lift up out of his chair and do a bull run toward the agent.

Sherwood pushed Vanessa to the floor and turned at the same instant Lou butted his head against Sherwood's chest. Sherwood's gun went off and Lou collapsed in a heap by Vanessa. She screamed and fell over her bleeding son.

"You've killed him," she shouted at Sherwood. "You've killed the wrong son, you idiot." The hatred in her dark eyes seared through the cloying humidity. She dragged herself up and started hitting at Sherwood.

Connor came out of his stupor and went into action. He rammed one of the big guards in the stomach and snatched the man's rifle, then slammed it against the giant's head. The man went down with a moan.

Josie saw that distraction and made her own by knocking her chair over so she could do a roll toward the now-confused other guard. He barreled toward Connor, but she leveled her body near his feet, causing him to trip and fall over her. When his handgun clattered to the floor, Josie grabbed it with her tied hands and held it near his head.

"Don't move," she said, her breath rasping with each word.

"You won't shoot me, lady," the big guy said on a smooth note.

"No, but they will." She motioned to the two even-bigger men who'd rushed through the door.

Mama Joe's men.

Her doubtful hostage glanced over his shoulder and let out a long sigh.

Josie kept the gun on him. "Now untie me before I decide I will shoot you just to prove a point."

He did as she asked and soon she was free. In the next few seconds, Mama Joe's men had secured the room and more of them had converged on the group to settle everyone back down. Two of them held Sherwood away from the still-screaming Vanessa Armond.

"It's over," Connor shouted to Sherwood, taking the pistol Big Toby handed him so he could hold it on Sherwood. "It's all over."

Sherwood shook his head and laughed. "You just think it's over. For once in his life, Armond told the truth. You are his son."

Josie came to stand beside Connor. "One of you had better tell me the truth, because I'm going to call the New Orleans Police Department and have you all hauled in."

Connor grabbed her and pulled her close. "Josie, I didn't know. I don't believe him," he said, shaking his head. "It's impossible."

"No, it's not," Vanessa said, her energy spent. She tugged past the posse and came to stand by Armond's bed. "It's a long story, but you need to hear it." She glanced down at Armond and their eyes met. "But first, can we please get my husband to a hospital?" Then she glanced back at where Lou lay in a pool of blood. "And . . . take my son's body away, please."

Two hours later, Josie sat spent and shocked in a conference room at the FBI building in New Orleans. She'd just been through one of the hardest hours of her life, having to explain why she'd brought their boss in wearing handcuffs, his face scratched and dirty, his gaze fevered with a certain rage that would never go away.

She wasn't sure she could do this job anymore.

The door opened and Connor came in with another agent and Vanessa Armond.

He sat down beside Josie, his demeanor shell-shocked, his mood somber.

"Okay, she's ready to talk," Agent Benton said in an I've-heard-it-all-now voice. His sharp-edged crew cut matched the set of his stubborn jaw and near-black eyes.

Josie nodded. She'd already given her statement and so had Connor. Armond was dehydrated and feverish but he was being treated in a nearby hospital. Lou was dead.

Now they had one last item of business to

take care of. Vanessa had promised to explain everything.

After Agent Benton went through the preliminaries, he sat back and stared at the older woman. "Okay, Mrs. Armond, let's hear your side of the story."

Vanessa lifted her eyes to Connor. "I knew your mother," she explained. "We were good friends when we were younger. She worked at one of the local hotels as an event coordinator and I'd come in with my boyfriend—Louis. We actually met with her to plan our wedding reception." She smiled but her eyes remained tattered and dark. "He was always the one for me." Then she shook her head. "But I wasn't always the one for him."

Connor glanced over at Josie and shook his head. "My mother loved this city, always. She traveled back and forth between here and England. But . . . my father was British. She always told me he was a British businessman."

"She lied," Vanessa said on a catlike hiss of breath. "They all lied."

"Let's get back to the facts," Josie said on a hoarse command. She didn't know who to believe, but she knew to follow the evidence. "Please continue."

Vanessa pushed at her thick sliver-streaked hair. "They had an affair." She shot Connor an accusing glance. "Your mother and my Louis—

they had an affair." She shrugged. "Louis married me to secure his future. My father was wealthy."

Connor finally sat up straight. "And my mother?"

"She went to England and . . . you were born."

"Did you know about Connor then?" Josie asked, her heart torn into pieces.

Vanessa shook her head. "I pretended I didn't know about the affair and I never knew about the pregnancy. But then you showed up here and Louis changed after that. He changed." She hit a hand on the table. "I hated you the day I saw you at my house, because I knew. I knew. You look just like he did at your age."

Josie closed her eyes and tried again. "So . . . how did Sherwood get involved in all of this?"

Vanessa's scowl brought out the wrinkles she'd tried so hard to hide. "Sherwood wanted to bring down the Armond empire." She laughed, her eyes dancing over Connor's face. "Your mother's shooting—that was no accident."

Connor came up off his chair. "Stop doing this. Stop making excuses for Armond and for yourself and just tell us the truth."

"That is the truth," Vanessa said, her tone low and level. "Agent Joseph Sherwood arrived in New Orleans when Louis and I had been married fifteen years. By then, your mother was a distant memory and we were fairly happy. I turned my head to my husband's philandering because by then we had Lou."

"Lou's the one," Connor said, his hands flailing out around him. "Lou's the only son. I don't believe any of this."

"Lou is the son of Louis Armond," Vanessa retorted, anger vibrating through her words. "Lou was his son, too. I had to protect my son." She lowered her head, tears falling down her face. "I was trying to protect my son."

"Go ahead," Agent Benton urged. "Let's go back to Mr. Randall's mother. What do you know about her being mugged and killed?"

Vanessa cleared her throat. "Sherwood immediately decided he wanted to bring down my husband, so he kept digging and digging and sending out his spies. He thoroughly researched our backgrounds and that's when he discovered Louis had had an affair with a woman named Opal Connor."

Connor put a hand to his forehead. "My mother."

"Yes, your mother," Vanessa replied. "I don't know how he found out, but he somehow managed to figure out my husband had an illegitimate son." She leaned over the table. "He questioned your mother, started harassing her to the point that he must have blackmailed her or threatened her. She called my husband, begging for help." Vanessa glared at Connor. "She even brought you here once, to show you off to Louis."

Connor went still again, his eyes a dark, swirling river.

Josie wanted to reach out to him, but she didn't know how to comfort him now. "Go on," she said to Mrs. Armond.

"Louis did what he could, but that only reinforced Sherwood's obsession. Sherwood planned to have your mother killed, hoping it would bring my husband to his knees."

Connor got up and went to the wall and placed his forehead against the painted concrete. "I don't believe any of this. My mother was mugged and robbed."

"Yes, I know," Vanessa said, her voice carrying across the room. "I read about it in the paper, but I knew exactly who'd orchestrated it. You see, my husband still loved your mother. And he was destroyed when he heard about her death."

"But not enough to give up," Connor said on a heated shout. "He kept on doing what he was so good at, right?"

"Yes," Vanessa replied. "But he watched over her orphans. Even after you left your little sister and turned to crime."

Connor whirled to stare at Vanessa. "No, he did not watch over us. You're lying. If he'd been my father, I wouldn't have lived in poverty. I wouldn't have been moved from home to home until I had to take my sister and get away."

Vanessa slumped in her chair. "Why would I lie now? It's over. My son is dead and my husband

271

is close to dying. I have nothing left. Louis had planned to leave the bulk of his estate to his first-born son—you. And he had the proof of Sherwood's dirty deeds recorded on that little card because he wanted revenge."

Josie put Connor's feeling aside so she could get to the truth. "So your husband lured Sherwood into some sort of deal, a partnership of sorts?"

Vanessa's cackle chilled the air. "No. I was the one who offered Sherwood something he couldn't resist. I went to him and told him what I've told you about the affair. I offered him money and information and . . . revenge." She smiled up at Connor. "I hired him to have your mother killed."

Connor came across the table at her, but Agent Benton and Josie both pulled him back.

"She's a monster," Connor shouted. "She's doing this to get even with me because . . . because . . ." He stopped, sat down on his chair. "Because Armond and I grew so close."

"Exactly," Vanessa said on a rasping breath. "Exactly." She put her head in her hands. "You've been serving your sentence here in New Orleans for a reason, Connor. For many reasons. And now you know all of them."

Agent Benton gave Josie a concerned glance. "We have the real SIM card and . . . we're analyzing it. We'll compare what we learn there to Sherwood's statement and to this information. I think I've got what I need here and I can finish this without you two." He nodded toward the door. "Agent Gilbert, why don't you take Mr. Randall for a walk?"

Josie didn't know how to handle this Connor. He was silent, dark and unyielding. Even with her.

"Connor?"

He walked ahead of her out in the back parking lot. Bright pink crape myrtles bloomed along a fence line, deceptively beautiful as they lifted out toward the afternoon sun.

"Connor, you're exhausted. You should get some rest."

He whirled on her, his eyes so dark, she thought of storm-tossed seas and sinking boats. "I do not need to rest. I need to find out the truth."

"We know the truth," she said. "We know everything now. It all makes sense. Armond took you under his wing, tried to help you. He didn't have a silent partner. Vanessa did. She was the one who brought Sherwood into their inner circle. I believe Armond was duped by both of them."

"And I was duped by all of them." He laughed, a cutting, ragged sound. "Me, Josie. The con man who's outsmarted both criminals and law-enforcement agents alike—I was such a fool, such a confused, misguided fool."

Josie could certainly identify with that. "I understand—"

He turned to stare at her. "No, you don't. My mother lied to me and withheld things, more now than I ever realized. She told me my father wanted nothing to do with us."

"Maybe she was trying to spare you."

"Spare me? The woman ruined my life."

"She didn't mean to die, Connor."

"No, but she forgot how to live. She wanted the life Armond had promised her, but all she managed to do was rack up bills and . . . leave me in debt. How can I ever explain this to Deidre?"

"What can I do to help you?" Josie asked, her heart buckling. "Connor, what?"

He grabbed her, held her there in front of him. "You can find a way to release me from the FBI. Because if you don't, I will leave, Josie. I'll just go and take my chances."

"And what about us?" she asked, tears gathering in spite of her tightly clenched jaw. "What about us, Connor?"

"Like you told me, there isn't any us. Maybe there never was."

He turned away before she could argue. Then he walked toward the high fence that stood between them and the flowering crape myrtles, his head down, his hands in the pockets of his jeans.

Josie waited for him to look back.

He never did.

Two months later
London, England

She had a visual. The little café on the corner gave Josie a perfect view of three different London streets. She knew Connor had been staying in a flat around the corner. Now she just had to wait for him to come to this little café for his morning coffee. So she sat sipping her own cappuccino and nibbling on a pastry while her heart did little dancing spasms of doubt coupled with anticipation.

He'd walked away.

From the FBI, from his father and from her.

Just like that.

The FBI had released him from his duties, citing his work to bring down former special agent in charge Joseph Sherwood and breaking up the Armond crime family for good.

The SIM card had verified what Vanessa and Sherwood himself had told them. And Armond had backed it up, giving his confession with a clear conscience and what seemed like a sigh of relief.

But he'd given Josie a message to his son. "Tell him I'm sorry and that I didn't know about him until his mother came back to ask for my help. I didn't know. I tried to make amends. I did."

Sherwood had purposely brought Connor to

New Orleans to lure Armond, but he'd withheld the truth out of fear that Connor would bolt to the other side.

Armond had called Connor to the opera house that night to warn him and to confess that Sherwood was in cahoots with Vanessa. He'd guessed who'd killed Lewanna and he was afraid Connor would be next. But Sherwood had made sure Armond wouldn't be able to talk to Connor. He'd shot Armond and faked his own injury before whisking Armond into hiding.

Sherwood had hoped to find the evidence and then kill all the principle players before Connor and Josie figured it out.

A man's career gone.

A father's love destroyed.

A son's heart broken.

And one former FBI agent sitting in a café in London waiting for the man she loved.

Josie leaned forward in her chair and wondered how Connor would react to seeing her again.

Before she could imagine that reunion, a strong hand came around her shoulder and held her mouth shut. "Don't make a sound."

She recognized that cultured, accented voice.

Connor.

She tried to glance over her shoulder, but his breath on her neck stopped her. "What do you want, Agent Gilbert?"

Josie wrestled herself around and turned to

stare up at him. "I want you, of course. And . . . that's *former agent* to you."

He let go of her and sank down beside her. "You quit?"

"Of course I quit. I had to bring down the man I worked for. Not very good for PR around the office."

Connor stared over at her, giving her a chance to see the blue of his eyes, the stubble of his shadow of a beard and . . . the trace of hope in his hardened expression. "I would think you'd receive a medal and a promotion."

"I was offered a promotion but I decided to try something new."

"And what's that?"

"Tracking down a wanted man."

He grabbed part of her pastry and chewed. "Me, a wanted man? Imagine that? Who wants me now?"

"Just me," she said on a shy smile. "Just me— unemployed and bored and . . . lonely me. I told you if you left I'd find you."

He drank most of her cappuccino before he gave her a blank stare. "What are you really doing here, Josie?"

Josie let out an exasperated sigh and reached a hand up to touch his face. "Trying to tell you that I love you," she finally said.

Connor's hand covered hers and drew it away from his face. "Are you sure? Because you sure didn't seem convinced about me, even after I told you I didn't know that Armond was my father."

"More than sure." She clutched her fingers against his. "Positively beyond-a-shadow-of-doubt sure."

He pulled away and gave her one of his blue-eyed gazes. "I had to get away to make *positively* sure I could handle things."

"Your father wants to see you."

He nodded. "I know. I'm still trying to work my way toward that meeting. Deidre prays for me on a daily basis."

"So do I," Josie replied.

Connor shot her a look of gratitude. "No wonder I feel so much better about things now."

"He's in prison," she said. "But he's resigned himself to that, I think. Someone once told me he had a heart underneath all that criminal activity."

"And maybe he does. He did give up a lot to come clean." Connor shrugged. "I'll go see him one day." He nudged her. "Hey, maybe we could swing by and visit your daddy, too."

"Touché," she said. "And for now?"

"I'm an almost millionaire," he quipped. "I didn't take any of the dirty money he wanted me to have. And I won't after he's gone, either." Then he grinned. "But I did keep the Camaro."

Josie thanked God for his new attitude. "Noble of you to let go of the fortune."

"It was the right thing to do." Looking away, he added, "I've been doing some consulting work and I'm actually getting paid." He turned back and stared over at her, a slow, soft smile cresting on his full lips. "So, former agent Josie Gilbert, what do you plan to do next?"

"Handcuff you and take you hostage," she retorted.

"No need for that," he replied. Then he lifted her out of her chair and danced her around the table. "Why don't we start with me showing you London and see how we do from there?"

Josie nodded. "I'd like that."

He tugged her close. "Now, repeat what you said earlier, please."

"Which part?"

"The part about you loving me."

"I love you," she said, her hand moving down his face.

Connor leaned down and kissed her. Then he whispered in her ear, "I love you, too. Even without the handcuffs."

Josie smiled into the kiss and thanked God for frequent-flyer points and . . . for allowing her to finally find the real Connor Randall.

Dear Reader,

Do you remember the movie *Catch Me if You Can*? It starred Leonardo DiCaprio as a con man who'd fooled a lot of people before turning to help the FBI. I've always been fascinated with that movie. So when Connor Randall—a reformed con artist—stepped onto the pages of *In Pursuit of a Princess*, I knew I'd have to write his story.

It was a tricky balance of showing his shady past while pushing him toward a complete redemption. Connor loves his baby sister, Deidre (who was also in my princess book), so he wants to redeem himself in her eyes. Deidre's strong faith has left a lasting impression on Connor, too. When he meets Special Agent Josie Gilbert and realizes she's the real deal, he also wants to show Josie that he's changed. But Josie has her own reasons for not trusting anyone, so she can't be conned or won over so easily.

I enjoyed this adventure with Connor and Josie and I hope you did, too. I believe there is good in all of us, so I'm glad Connor found his true calling and that he fell in love. I hope you will remember that no matter what you have in your past, God is always there ready to listen and stand by you.

Until next time, may the angels watch over you. Always.

Leona Worth

Questions for Discussion . . .

1. Connor Randall is a different kind of inspirational hero. Was it easy for you to accept him or did you have doubts about him?

2. Josie was a rookie who already felt guilty about a botched assignment. Do you think it was fair that she was saddled with a recovering con artist?

3. Connor held his secrets close to his heart, but he wanted to be a better person for his sister's sake. Did you believe he was sincere?

4. Josie had some issues with her past and a father who lied and cheated. Do you believe this is why she pushed Connor away?

5. What did you see as the overall theme of this story? The word *redemption* kept popping into my mind, but I think it went deeper than that. Forgiveness of one's self has to come with redemption, don't you think?

6. Why do you think Connor almost felt sorry for Louis Armond? Do you believe they were real friends or just playing a game?

7. Why couldn't Connor get the goods on Armond?

8. Josie thought he was protecting the aging gangster. Did you believe that at first?

9. Josie loves her job but she values honesty above all else. Was she being too rigid in dealing with that?

10. Louis Armond had a mansion, but spiritually, he had nothing. Have you ever known someone who thought they had it all only to realize they needed God in their lives?

11. Why did Connor and Josie feel so safe at Mama Joe's? Have you ever found an unusual quiet shelter from life's woes?

12. In the end, Armond tried to make up for his mistakes. Do you think he got what he deserved?

13. In the end, Connor paid dearly for the life he'd chosen. Do you think he'll be able to overcome the secrets revealed at the end?

14. Josie could have turned on Connor but she chose to believe in him. Why did she think he'd do the right thing?

15. Being a law-enforcement person can bring burnout and a jaded sense of justice. Have you ever had to deal with someone who's given up on life?

16. Do you think Deidre should have her own book? What would you like to see happen with her?

About the Author . . .

Leona Worth has written more than forty books for three different publishers. Her career with Love Inspired Books spans close to fifteen years. In February 2011 her Love Inspired Suspense novel *Body of Evidence* made the *New York Times* bestseller list. Her very first Love Inspired title, *The Wedding Quilt*, won *Affaire de Coeur*'s Best Inspirational for 1997, and *Logan's Child* won an *RT Book Reviews* Best Love Inspired for 1998. With millions of books in print, Lenora continues to write for the Love Inspired and Love Inspired Suspense lines. Lenora also wrote a weekly opinion column for the local paper and worked freelance for years with a local magazine. She has now turned to full-time fiction writing and enjoying adventures with her retired husband, Don. Married for thirty-six years, they have two grown children. Lenora enjoys writing, reading and shopping . . . especially shoe shopping.

Center Point Large Print
600 Brooks Road / PO Box 1
Thorndike, ME 04986-0001 USA

(207) 568-3717

US & Canada:
1 800 929-9108
www.centerpointlargeprint.com